On the Move
Soldiering On Security #6

Aislinn Kearns

Copyright © 2018 Aislinn Kearns
All rights reserved.
ISBN-13: 9781983052682

Other books by the Author:

Underground Fighters Series

Caged Warrior
Russian Beast
Undercover Fighter

CONTENTS

Chapter One	1
Chapter Two	11
Chapter Three	23
Chapter Four	44
Chapter Five	62
Chapter Six	87
Chapter Seven	107
Chapter Eight	128
Chapter Nine	147
Chapter Ten	162
Chapter Eleven	184
Chapter Twelve	193
Chapter Thirteen	204
Chapter Fourteen	220
Chapter Fifteen	231
Chapter Sixteen	243

CHAPTER ONE

The wind from the open plane door whipped at his face. Beneath him, the canopy of a vast rainforest lit by moonlight stretched endlessly into the distance, past where even his excellent vision could see.

Almost there.

Mike tested the straps on his parachute for the hundredth time. It had been a few years since he'd done a jump, but muscle memory should take over once he was in the air. Maybe he should've done a few simple test jumps first, before going straight to the highest level of difficulty. Treejumps were the most dangerous.

Still, he'd be fine. Hopefully.

The pilot—his friend and colleague, Charlie—waved one hand to get his attention. The other stayed locked on the controls, keeping the shuddering plane steady. They'd hired the piece of shit aircraft when they'd arrived in Zolego, the South American country they now flew above. It was the best they could find, but that wasn't saying much.

"We're coming up on the drop site. You ready?" Charlie asked, turning enough for Mike to read his lips by the flickering internal light of the plane.

Mike gave a thumbs up. "Always," he yelled back.

"See you in about twelve hours," Charlie said with a grin.

Mike nodded. Anticipation roared through him. His palms dampened and his heart thumped in his chest. He'd missed this.

He stuck one hand in his pocket and rubbed his finger over the coin he kept there. A good luck charm, as well as a reminder of different times, when Mike had done jumps like this regularly, with a different team by his side. When he'd still had his hearing and his best friend.

Charlie peered out of the window to his left, then gave a thumbs up over his shoulder. Mike launched himself out of the plane without hesitation, shaking off the melancholy mood that always hit him when he thought about Ramirez.

Then, he was falling.

He grinned. The familiar sensation of plummeting towards Earth was like coming home. He closed his eyes for a brief moment, reveling in the sensation of the wind plastering his jacket to his chest. Then, he snapped them open. He couldn't get complacent. He was here to do a job, and the jump could kill him if he wasn't careful.

He tugged on the tab to release his parachute. It burst out, yanking him violently into a drift. Mike took a deep breath and surveyed the area.

He spotted his destination—a rebel camp—a few clicks away. If all went well, he'd reach it before dawn.

The canopy came up fast, even with his descent slowed by the parachute, a result of jumping from a low altitude. He tugged at the controls, gliding towards his landing site. As planned, the moon hung on the opposite side of the sky, so it wouldn't cast him in shadow over the camp. He still hoped no one looked up.

He made a final adjustment, then braced for impact as his feet brushed the canopy. He crashed through the treetops with violent force. Branches, leaves, and God knew what else whacked at him. Pain stung his arm as a sharp offshoot scraped him. He'd be hurting tomorrow.

Finally, the parachute snagged on something and he jerked to a halt. He took half a second to breathe in relief as he swung from the momentum of his fall. It hadn't been his smoothest landing, but considering it was his first in a long time, he'd take it.

Heart still pounding with adrenaline, Mike reached up to tug at the parachute above him. Secure.

Then, he looked down.

And saw nothing.

Mike waited for his eyes to adjust, but nope. The moonlight simply didn't penetrate that far down. He couldn't see the ground beneath him to estimate how far up he was. No surprise, given how tall the trees were and how thick the canopy.

Well, he hoped it was less than thirty meters down, since that was all the rope he had. If not…he'd figure something out.

Mike twisted behind him and pulled out the heavy rope. Holding it carefully, since he'd be screwed if he dropped it, he found the end. He looped it through the descender at his waist and then attached it to the risers of his parachute as an anchor. Before he let go, he tested both the parachute and the rope would hold his weight.

It held steady.

Mike exhaled, then dropped the end into the darkness below.

Keeping a firm hold on the rope, Mike unclipped himself from the parachute. He swallowed, then descended into the darkness.

His eyesight got progressively worse as he went farther down, until he couldn't see a thing. Mike was deaf, had been since an explosion in Iraq damaged his eardrums, so the lack of sight made him more vulnerable than he'd been in a long time. He reached out to plant a hand against the enormous trunk of the tree he hung from, orienting himself using the rough bark beneath his fingertips.

Faint shapes appeared out of the darkness. His eyes were finally adjusting.

He was nearly at the end of the rope, so at least he could—vaguely—see where he'd drop to.

He eased off his pack and threw it to the side. When it hit the ground, some creature he couldn't identify scurried away from the noise. Hopefully nothing deadly that would come back and bite him on the ass later. Literally.

Mike lowered himself down until his hands gripped the very end of the rope.

He let go.

And landed with a bone-jarring thud.

He bent his knees to absorb some of the impact and rolled head over ass in the springy earth to distribute the rest of the force. His teeth rattled, but he'd take it. He'd made it back to Earth safely.

Mike allowed himself a brief moment of relief, then stood. He had a mission to complete, and the hardest part was still to come.

He hefted his pack onto his shoulders. The rope still dangled where he left it. He hated leaving it behind, but there was no way to get it down. He also dropped his jacket—unnecessary in the oppressive heat beneath the canopy—and the harness with the descender on it. He needed to travel light.

He took out his compass and a pocket flashlight to double check his directions, then headed off into the undergrowth. As he went, he unsheathed his kukri blade to hack his way past the worst of the plants, slicing at vines, branches, oversized leaves, and anything else that got in his way. The long, curved blade had a dull sheen in the weak moonlight.

He moved quickly, and as quietly as he could manage, considering he couldn't hear his own footsteps. He didn't want to disturb the locals of either the human or animal varieties. He kept the flashlight on, though, determined not to run into anything nasty. His mission could be over before it began if he wasn't careful. The undergrowth was thick enough that it should hide the light from anyone until they were right on top of him.

The glow of firelight finally appeared in the distance. He sheathed his kukri blade as he crept closer, in case the noise attracted attention.

A hastily-constructed fence loomed over him, twice his height. Torches made from branches and rags dotted the fence to scare off animal predators. They wouldn't be expecting a human predator this deep in the jungle.

Mike backed into the shadows and carefully shimmied up a tree to see over the fence. He was careful where he put his hands and feet, both to avoid any dangerous creatures, and to limit the noise he made. Hopefully, the rebels in the compound would think it was a panther or other large animal if they heard him, but he didn't want to take any unnecessary risks.

Not until he had the target with him, anyway.

The compound was small, maybe enough for thirty people to comfortably walk around. It was constructed entirely of wood, and not designed to be a permanent structure. To the left, there were five one-room buildings. In the center, a large fire, likely for cooking.

The camp was quiet given the early hour. Dawn was still an hour away. A few rebels stood at even intervals around the camp, semi-automatic rifles held loosely in their hands. They weren't expecting trouble. One guy dragged on a cigarette. Two friends chatted in the shadows.

Mike would prefer no guards at all, but he'd take non-vigilant ones over professionals any day.

To his right, was another small building, no different from the others. Except this one had two guards stationed out front.

That was his destination. It had to be.

The building had no windows, so Mike couldn't see what was inside, but surely they'd only post guards if the contents of the room was worth money to them.

Now, the question was how to liberate their prisoner without alerting the guards.

If he had the time, he'd watch the rebels to discover their schedule. It would be much easier to help a prisoner escape during the relative chaos of a guard change, but Mike didn't know when that would be. And he couldn't wait, because every second she was in there was a second she was in danger.

Dawn was coming, and he needed her out of the compound before then.

He needed a distraction.

Mike leaned over to pluck a torch from its holder. None of the guards noticed.

He dropped to the ground and circled the fence until he found the perfect spot for his distraction. He held the burning torch to the fence until the flames caught, radiating heat, then immediately rounded the compound until he was behind the building acting as a prison.

It didn't take the rebels long to notice the fire. Mike could see their panicked movements between the fence spikes as the guards scrambled to find enough water to put it out. If the fire got too out of control with this much burnable wood around, the entire rainforest could be in trouble.

Mike forced the guilt aside. He had to focus on getting Jessica Vanderslice to safety. As long as the fire burned long enough to distract them, it would do its job.

Mike tore the fence spikes from the ground. He peered through the gap he'd made, but no one raced towards him.

His heart pounded with adrenaline. He loved missions; loved their energy, loved the challenge. More challenging since he'd been medically discharged, but that made it all the more exhilarating.

Mike squeezed through the gap he'd made. He hesitated a moment. The door to the hut was around the front, in full view of the rebels. Should he risk it, and hope they were distracted enough by the fire not to notice? Or should he tear a hole in the back of the rickety hut, which they might hear anyway?

He opted for speed over invisibility. He didn't want to waste his distraction.

Mike slid around the side of the building, staying in the shadows as much as possible. When the rebels' backs were turned, he sprinted the few remaining steps and slipped inside. He closed the door behind him, leaving an inch open so he could peer through the gap. No one moved towards him.

Perfect.

He turned to the room's other occupant. The only illumination in the room came from the cracks in the hastily-constructed wall, which let in the flickering firelight. And, yep, he'd been right.

Jessica Vanderslice sat on a poorly constructed wooden chair. Her hands were bound behind her, and fabric was stretched across her mouth to keep her quiet. She wore cargo pants and a loose linen shirt over a tank top, but none of her clothes looked like they'd been washed in weeks. He couldn't see much of her features in the dull light, but enough to form an impression. Dark hair hung limp and matted around her dirt-smeared face.

But the dirt did nothing to detract from her beauty.

She had the kind of face that spoke of centuries of good breeding. Her mother, Senator Vanderslice, came from a family with a long and venerated history, and it showed in every line of Jessica's delicate face. Her father was one of the last Vanderslices born into the family's vast fortune. It made Mike want to sneer, at the money and the breeding, and all the things he hated about rich, privileged people. But her face also wanted to make him fall to his knees and pledge loyalty, like a knight of old swearing fealty to a lady.

The thought made Mike even more annoyed, so he ignored it.

Instead, he focused on the woman. He'd taken in the sight of her in seconds, his military training having taught him to observe situations at a glance.

He stepped forward and said, "I'm here to rescue you."

At least, that's what he *would* have said.

If she hadn't taken that moment to kick him in the nuts.

CHAPTER TWO

"Fuck."

Jessica winced. The man was American. When he'd come in, all huge and intimidating, she'd simply reacted. Hadn't considered he might be on her side.

She couldn't even apologize, gagged as she was. Instead, she scrunched her face in sympathy as the big man glared at her. He hadn't gone down with her kick, but he breathed heavily through the pain.

"What I was *going* to say," he growled. "Was 'don't panic, I'm here to rescue you' but it looks like you've got that part covered."

Jessica narrowed her eyes. She apologized, but the gag garbled the words. Was he really blaming her for instinctively lashing out at a huge man coming towards her while she was tied up and vulnerable? She knew men were precious about their nuts, but really.

He stepped forward, arm reaching towards her, and Jessica flinched back, heart pounding. He paused, then moved slower. She didn't freak out this time as he hooked a finger into her mouth and dragged the gag out.

"Thank you," she choked out, mouth painfully dry from the lack of water and the gag soaking up what little moisture remained.

He ignored her. "We have to go."

She nodded enthusiastically, then twisted to show him her hands were bound to the chair behind her. He yanked a knife from his belt. Jessica swallowed at the sight of the blade.

He stepped behind her. With both speed and care, he sliced through the braided vines binding her. As soon as they were no longer wrapped tightly around her wrist, all the blood flowed back into her limbs, stabbing pain through her shoulders, arms, and hands.

She shook her arms to get feeling back, even as she focused on her rescuer. "What's your name?" she whispered, conscious of the guards outside. Distant yelling reached her, but it wasn't clear enough for her to understand what they said.

The rebels' panic was clear, though. What had her rescuer done to distract them? Was it something to do with the flickering light coming through the cracks?

He didn't reply. Instead, he pulled her to her feet and gave her a once-over. Checking for injuries, she assumed. There wasn't any blatant male appreciation in the gaze, which she was both appreciative of and disappointed by. She felt like a disgusting swamp monster, since she hadn't bathed properly in over a week, and the rainforest made her sweat constantly.

But even though Jessica was the dirtiest human in the world right now—and not in the good way—she had to admit she wouldn't mind a guy like this checking her out. He was tall and solidly built beneath his army-green t-shirt. The low light in this hut did nothing to disguise those muscles.

His face was strong, too. Not handsome, exactly, but compelling. Harsh planes softened by laugh lines. His expression was intense now, focused. He was on a mission. And Jessica couldn't help but imagine what it would be like to be the subject of all that focus.

But now wasn't the time to think about that. Not while he strode to the door to peek out into the compound of rebels. The noise outside had increased in the last few minutes, the panic reaching fever pitch.

Whatever her rescuer saw outside, it made him yank open the door. Two rebels stumbled to a stop, staring at him in shock. They didn't raise their guns, or yell, too surprised to see a large American man in their midst.

Her rescuer didn't hesitate, though. He strode two steps forward and then used his large hands to whack the two men's heads together.

They dropped like stones.

Her rescuer—damn it, what was his name?—wrenched the semi-automatics from their loose grips and slung one of the straps over his shoulder. He turned and held the other one out to her.

"Know how to use this?"

Jessica blinked. "Sort of?"

He gave a sharp nod. "Good enough. Just point and shoot if you need to, but not at me."

So, he was still sour about the nut shot. Well, it served him right for looming over her without introducing himself.

"Sure," she said, but didn't intend to do any such thing. She wasn't a killer.

Jessica looped the strap over her neck and pointed the barrel at the ground. She'd only held one of these things a couple of times, and never by choice.

She hated guns.

"Don't shoot the rebels if you can help it," she pleaded.

"What?" he asked, confused as if he hadn't heard her right.

"Don't shoot them," she repeated, gesturing to the rebels beyond that were still focused on—Jesus, where had that fire come from? It was huge, roaring up the trunk of an ancient tree. Jessica swallowed. That wouldn't end well.

But even as she watched, more of the rebels came over with buckets of water, forming an assembly line between them and the place they stored the food and water. They'd be able to put it out, as long as they didn't run out of liquid.

"Why not?" her rescuer asked.

"They aren't bad people, they're desperate."

"They *kidnapped* you," he reminded her.

"Yes. But only because they need the money from the ransom to support their cause."

He nodded as if he already knew that. "Do *you* support their cause?"

She hesitated. "I think anyone would be better than the current regime," she hedged.

He narrowed his eyes. "Did you get kidnapped on purpose?" he asked incredulously.

"No! Of course not," she protested. "I simply understand why they did it."

He raised an eyebrow at her. She thought he might argue, but then shook his head in an exasperated gesture. "Do you even want to get rescued?"

"Of course."

"Good. Then follow me."

He turned away, surveying the camp.

"Hey, what's your name?" Jessica demanded.

He ignored her once again, striding around the side of the building. Jessica hesitated for a brief moment, watching the rebels and the fire which was slowly growing smaller, but then she hurried after her rescuer.

She was almost at the corner of the hut when a shout of warning went up. They'd spotted her. She quickened her pace, sprinting after her rescuer where he slipped through a gap in the fence. He wasn't hurrying. Not until he glanced over her shoulder and his eyes widened.

As Jessica pushed through the gap, brushing against the tall American's hard body as she did so, she took the opportunity to look back.

Half the rebels were still battling the fire. The other half ran towards them, raising their semi-automatics. Jessica's heart jumped. The fence wouldn't protect them from bullets.

General Moreno stepped from the shadows to stand in front of his men. He was a tall man, in good shape, with an aura of gravitas. She'd encountered him a few times in her week there, when he visited to ask her disconnected questions she didn't always understand.

He was the leader of the rebels. And if he and his men got their way, he'd be the new ruler of Zolego before the year was out.

Their eyes met, and a cold shiver went down Jessica's spine at the fury there. He'd gone to a lot of trouble to arrange her kidnapping, and now she was slipping away.

He held up a hand to his men and barked an order in Portuguese. Her limited understanding of the language told her that it was an order not to fire their weapons. Jessica's brow tugged down in confusion.

Then, Moreno and his men advanced as one, striding towards Jessica. His gaze was focused on her, freezing her to the spot. Even her breath stilled in her lungs.

The American held up the assault rifle he carried and fired a stream of bullets near the rebels. They ducked, all except Moreno, who seemed unconcerned. He must have somehow known that the bullets were intentionally fired wide, a fact Jessica was grateful for.

Jessica's rescuer stopped shooting and grabbed her hand, startling her from her staring contest with Moreno. He dragged her the rest of the way through the fence and into the rainforest beyond. She stumbled, then righted herself, conscious of the rebels behind her. The crunching of her feet on the forest floor as they ran drowned any sounds of pursuit there might have been. She was tempted to look back, but didn't want to trip on the undergrowth and slow them down.

Jessica's breath sawed painfully in her lungs and her head swum. She hadn't slept, eaten or drunk properly in a week, making her tired and weak. But she determinedly continued forward.

Before long it grew almost unbearably dark beneath the trees as the fire got farther and farther away. But her rescuer didn't stop, didn't pause except to pull out a long blade, like a curved sword. He used it to hack at the worst of the undergrowth they encountered. But mostly he plowed through it, taking the brunt of the impact on his body.

Finally, he slowed to a stop beneath a large fern. Jessica gratefully stopped, too, panting. He pulled out a flashlight and clicked it on, then shone it right on her face.

"Can you hear any sounds of pursuit?" he asked.

She shut her eyes, partially against the glare, and partially to focus on her ears. After a long moment, she shook her head. "No."

The light left her face and she snapped her eyes open in time to see her rescuer nod in satisfaction.

"Tell me if you do."

He crouched at her feet, kneeling in the squishy mud beneath them. The ferns had collected water and concentrated it into a small puddle. Her rescuer had the flashlight between his teeth, pointing at his hands as he scooped them into the earth. Jessica frowned in confusion. What the hell…?

Her confusion changed to outrage as he stood and slapped the mud on her face.

"What the fuck?" she yelled.

"It's the best I can do for the moment to keep mosquitoes off you," he explained, smearing the mud over the exposed skin of her face, neck, and chest even as Jessica squirmed out of reach. His touch was clinical, impersonal, but it still made her heart race.

"I can live with a few bites," she muttered.

He paused. "Mosquito bites can be deadly out here. Malaria, Zika virus, all kinds."

Jessica's stomach churned. The rebels hadn't given her anything to keep the bugs off. She'd been fastidious about bug spray right up until she'd been kidnapped. Then, all protection stopped.

"I had all my shots," she said weakly as he continued smearing the mud. But she knew there was no immunization against Zika.

Her rescuer didn't answer her, kneeling to smear mud over himself, too. Once done, he didn't stand. Instead, he took off his pack and yanked out an old shirt.

Jessica jumped as he tore it into strips, the sound of the fabric ripping echoing into the darkness. She peered around, half-expecting to see rebels leap from the trees, but there was only the usual sounds of the night beyond whatever the American was doing. He set the strips of fabric aside and turned to tear large chunks of bark from the nearest tree. He pressed the bark against her shin and calf, surrounding the lower half of her left leg.

Jessica stepped back and placed her boot against his shoulder to hold him back. He looked up at her with a raised eyebrow and swung the flashlight with his jaw so the beam landed in her face.

"What are you doing now?" she asked. The mud was drying on her skin, tightening it uncomfortably like the world's worst facemask. She wanted to scratch it off, but the thought of getting the Zika virus kept her hands by her side.

Her rescuer sighed. "Just trust me. We don't have much time."

Jessica glanced back into the darkness in the direction she'd last seen Moreno. He was undoubtedly coming after her, considering what she represented for him and his cause. And she didn't want to go back to that hut, not for anything. She wanted safety, freedom, and a really hot shower.

And her rescuer was her best chance of making that happen. Despite his terrible manners, she had to trust him.

She removed her foot from his shoulder and stepped back into his reach. Without hesitating, he tied strips at her ankles and knees, over the bark, plastering her cargo pants to her leg.

When all that was done, he dug into his pack and pulled out two items Jessica had never seen before. It wasn't until he strapped them to his lower legs that she noticed they were the professionally made version of what he'd created for her with the bark.

When he was done, he stood and hefted the pack onto his back once more.

"Ready?" he asked, shining the light on her face again.

Jessica shielded her eyes. "What the hell are these things for?" she asked, pointing at her shin.

"So no deadly spiders, leeches, or other kinds of bugs get in there. They like warmth and skin."

Jessica swallowed and nodded. She'd always stuck to more populated areas of the country during her numerous visits here. When the rebels had kidnapped her from the orphanage she'd been volunteering in, they'd taken her to their stronghold deep in the forest. Government forces had driven them out of everywhere else, leaving only the depths of the Amazon as a safe hideout.

She'd never had to consider the deadly wildlife too much in the cities. But, now, she knew she had to, in the depths of the untouched parts of the Amazon.

"Why do you get the good ones?" she asked.

"Too big for you," he replied.

She nodded. That made sense. He obviously had his own equipment he'd brought with him, that didn't include lady-sized…whatever the hell these things were called. Shin guards?

He turned away at her nod. The patch of rainforest they'd been standing in was no longer so dark. Dawn wasn't far off.

Jessica frowned at her rescuer's back. "What's your name?" she asked for the third time. He ignored her once again, still continuing forward.

Jessica jogged forward. When she caught up, she took hold of his arm and wrenched him around. He gave her a confused look, then shined the light on her face. He was doing it to annoy her, she was sure.

She held a hand up to shield her eyes, then growled, "Why do you keep ignoring me?"

"What was the question?"

She rolled her eyes, teeth grinding. "What's your name?" Would it be fourth time lucky and she'd get her answer?

"Mike," he said simply. "Mike Ford."

"Was that really so hard?" she snarked. Then, she took a deep breath, pushing down her annoyance. She reminded herself that this man was her rescuer, and she needed him onside to get out of this place alive. She held out her hand. "Nice to meet you, Mike."

He took her hand in his, engulfing it, and shook. His palm was warm and strong against hers.

"Nice to meet you, Jessica." His voice was low and rough, causing a shiver to run down her spine.

He disentangled their hands. "I wasn't ignoring you, by the way."

"What?" she asked, focusing on Mike's words, not on how inconveniently attractive she found him.

"I wasn't ignoring you, I couldn't hear you." When she stared at him in confusion, he elaborated. "I'm deaf."

CHAPTER THREE

"Deaf," she repeated.

"That's right," he replied, unconcerned. Only his eyes were visible behind the mud he'd applied, having the added effect of blending his formerly-pale face into the darkness of the rainforest.

"How are you understanding me?"

"I'm reading your lips." He turned to leave and she grabbed his hand.

"Sorry. I'm not being mean, but you have to explain more. Who are you? I thought you were military, but if you're deaf..." she trailed off. "And you'd have a team, too." It finally occurred to her that it was strange that he'd come alone. They'd sent one guy to face off against a small army of rebels?

She'd trusted him because he was American, and because he'd focused on rescuing her. But perhaps she'd been wrong to jump to conclusions.

"I *was* in the military. A paratrooper. Until this." He waved his hands near his ears. "Now, I work for a private company called Soldiering On Security. Your parents hired us to get you home safe."

She swallowed. "My parents? Really?"

She didn't know why it surprised her, and yet it did. She'd half-expected them to leave her to the rebels, as punishment for what they saw as her disobedience. They'd never approved of her choices since she refused to go to law school.

"Yep," he confirmed.

"And they only sent you?" She eyed him suspiciously. "One man?"

"Yes. I was the only one with the experience at treejumping." He glanced behind them, eyes concerned. "I can explain it all later, but we have to get moving."

"But…"

"Is anyone coming?" he asked, then fell silent.

Jessica was tempted to keep pressing him for answers, but the reminder that they were likely being followed made adrenaline rush through her, and her heart pounded with the urge to flee. She closed her eyes and focused her hearing back in the direction they'd come from. Past the sleepy sounds of birds, the rustling of animals in the undergrowth, and the steady drip of water from close by, distant sounds reached her. Vines being viciously hacked, men shouting. All muffled by the oppressive force of the rainforest around them. It was impossible to say how far away they were.

Her eyes snapped open, and she again squinted against the glare of the flashlight. But she wasn't tempted to complain, now she knew he couldn't read her lips without it.

"They're coming," she told him. "But I don't think they're close."

He nodded once as if this was the answer he expected. "We'll have to move fast. I'll lead the way. If you need to get my attention, throw something at me. Don't feel bad, doesn't matter what it is. Just do it, since we need to be efficient and don't have time for pride. Okay?"

She swallowed, thinking of the men and the guns behind them, and the unknown darkness ahead. Only, it wasn't so dark anymore. The sun had started to rise while they'd been talking, shining a muted light on the world beneath the thick canopy above. Thank God. She hadn't relished plunging into the jungle, unable to see where she put her feet.

She eyed Mike. He didn't appear concerned about traversing the rainforest with one of his senses missing. He bounced impatiently on his toes, waiting for her to show him she was ready.

"Where are we going?" she asked.

"There's an airport about a day's hike from here. If we hustle, we can get there before dark. My friend, Charlie, made a deal for them to let him land the plane he's hired. We only get one shot, though, so we better get there fast."

"And then you'll take me home?" Her voice came out far smaller than she'd like, almost childlike. All through her ordeal of being kidnapped, the long car ride, the trek through the jungle, she'd stayed strong. She hadn't shown any weakness to her captors. They hadn't indicated any particular desire to hurt her, but she hadn't known if that would change—particularly if her parents refused to pay the ransom, which had been a very real possibility. No matter what, she hadn't let herself break down.

But now the possibility of home was very real, a tangible thing within her grasp. A day's walk and she'd be on her way. The force of her want almost choked her. The comfort of home. A soft bed instead of a chair. A hot shower. And her parents pampering and coddling her. Not that they were ever inclined to do that, since they'd never been the warmest parents. But after what she'd been through, the fantasy was nice.

Mike apparently hadn't noticed her moment of weakness, because he nodded impatiently. "Back to the US."

She felt a brief pang at his words, but followed Mike as he slid into the undergrowth, hacking and chopping only when they reached impenetrable barriers of vines and bush. Clearly, Mike knew his survivalist stuff, which Jessica appreciated. Her parents had chosen her rescuer well.

She stared at the broad breadth of his shoulders as they walked.

Would she ever come back to Zolego? The country had been good to her, for the most part. Welcoming, caring. And she knew she'd done some good here, through her charity work and volunteering. She'd partnered with many local organizations to bring everything from medical care to education to the neediest in the country, employing locals at every step.

But she didn't know if she could return after being kidnapped and held against her will. It wasn't the fault of the people she'd helped. It was the rebels in the country. Even though she understood their motives, she didn't approve of their actions. The Zolegan government was corrupt. She'd experienced that first hand, having to pay off numerous officials to continue her work, and even then they often still stood in her way.

She didn't hate the rebels for kidnapping her. They'd been desperate, and they no doubt believed the ends justified the means. The money from her ransom could have funded their rebellion for a year, allowing them to make real inroads against the government with a stranglehold on the nation. A government with immense power.

But Jessica couldn't quite forgive them for it, either.

Intellectually, she understood. Emotionally, she was furious.

She didn't want to punish the people of Zolego she'd been helping because of the rebels' actions, but she still didn't know if she could ever return to finish her work.

At least she didn't have to decide now. She shouldn't even be thinking it.

She needed to focus on getting out of here first, then think about the future. Even if she didn't come back to Zolego, there were plenty of other places that needed her help. Her heart sank, figuring most of them would be equally dangerous or unstable. She'd always known it was a risk, doing what she did. But the threat hadn't seemed real until it actually happened.

And now she was trekking through the jungle behind a man she didn't know, hoping to get home safely. Once she was there, she'd need to reevaluate her whole life. If she wasn't brave enough to keep volunteering like this, what would she do? Work for her mother's campaign?

She snorted. Not a chance.

Jessica stumbled, snapping her out of her thoughts. Mike didn't notice, so Jessica righted herself and kept going. But her head swam as she straightened.

What was wrong with her? Had the mosquitoes Mike mentioned got to her? Her heart skipped a beat in panic. Surely she wasn't sick? She didn't remember getting bitten, but would she have noticed?

Wait, when was the last time she'd eaten anything? She couldn't remember, which clued her in to the most likely cause of her dizziness. She came to a stop, breathing hard. Sweat beaded her face, making the mud mask slide over her skin. The air was like being wrapped in a humid cloud, and she struggled to suck the thick air into her lungs.

"Mike," she called softly, but of course he didn't notice.

She glanced around, spotting low-hanging fruit a few feet away. She yanked one off the tree and lobbed it towards him, landing it perfectly between his shoulder blades.

He immediately whipped around. When he caught sight of her his face changed from questioning to concerned. He jogged over.

"Are you okay?" he asked, eyeing her. He didn't need the flashlight now. The sun had fully risen, illuminating the rainforest even through the thick canopy above. She could now see the gigantic trees shooting towards the sky above them, the detail on the ferns behind Mike, and—

"Is that a spider?" she asked, momentarily forgetting her hunger. It was as big as her hand and furry.

He turned. "Yes. Not a deadly one though."

Jessica stumbled back, keeping an eye on the spider. She didn't know if they jumped, but she wasn't about to take the risk. At least it wasn't a snake.

She hated snakes.

She tore her gaze from the spider and met Mike's gaze. "I'm sorry, I need a break." Her gaze was drawn back to the creature behind him, but it wasn't particularly interested in the humans standing below it.

"Sure. Can you hear anyone?"

She shut her eyes and listened again, then shook her head. Either they were farther behind them, or they'd taken a different route. Hopefully, Mike's would be the fastest. Besides, there were only two of them, which would be faster to move than a whole rebel army.

Mike glanced up, then took his pack off and dropped it on the ground with a thud. Without warning, he launched himself into the nearest tree. She blinked in surprise. He climbed, faster than she would have believed possible. He must have crazy arm strength. She licked her dry lips as her imagination went into overdrive.

When he reached his destination, he wrapped his thick thighs around a branch and leaned out. His hand closed around the fruit hanging from a tree next to the one he'd climbed, about thirteen feet into the air. He tugged off a couple of them and pocketed them. Then, he clambered back down. The whole thing only took about a minute or two.

Jessica was reluctantly impressed.

Mike dug into his pocket and pulled out one of the fruits. He cut it in half with his kukri blade and then handed her one side. She took it gratefully.

"Papaya?" she asked.

He nodded. "It's the best food to get around here. You can eat it straight off the tree. No boiling or fussing required."

"Fussing?" she asked, amused. It wasn't a word she'd associate with a man like Mike. He seemed far too macho for that kind of thing. But maybe he had hidden depths.

She bit into the papaya as he made a face.

"You know what I mean. A lot of plants only have certain parts that are edible. You have to extract tiny seeds or strip them, cook them, that kind of thing. *Fussing.*"

"Right," she said on a laugh.

Apparently, Mike was the kind of guy that liked things easy and straightforward. It didn't surprise her, but it did make her curious about her rescuer. What else didn't she know?

"How long were you in the military?" she asked. Long enough to learn some impressive skills, she'd gather.

"Ten years, give or take," he replied, then took a huge bite of his papaya. The white juice ran down his chin and he mopped it up with his thumb as he chewed. Jessica's eyes followed the movement, oddly mesmerized by the sight of his strong jaw, dusted with stubble.

She took her own bite of fruit to distract herself from the heated thoughts. The sweetness was refreshing, knocking her mind out of the weird headspace it was in. She was dizzy from lack of food, that was all.

"And the...deafness?" she asked hesitantly, making sure to keep the fruit away from her mouth so he could read her lips. His eyes locked, so intently it made her breath catch. His focused gaze made her insides still, as if her whole body waited for him to do something. Like kiss her.

She shook her head to dismiss the mad idea.

He was silent for a second, and Jessica wondered briefly if she'd been insensitive about his deafness. She was usually much smoother—she was a politician's daughter, after all—but between her hunger and her strange reaction to Mike, she clearly wasn't on the top of her game.

But then he shrugged. "About three years ago. It was an IED. Went off right near me."

"I'm sorry," Jessica said, brows pulling down in sympathy.

"It's okay. I only lost my hearing, which isn't so bad. A lot of my men lost their lives that day." Shadows darkened his eyes. Despite the casual way he talked about it, he wasn't unaffected by his experience.

"I'm so sorry. Did you lose friends?"

"Yeah." He half-turned his body away, indicating he had no desire to continue that line of conversation. She grasped around for another question.

"And then you found Soldiering On Security?" she asked, to pull him out of wherever he'd gone in his mind. His eyes were vague, no longer focused on her lips.

"Hmmm?" he asked, returning his attention to her with a clear effort of will.

"You found work with Soldiering On Security?"

"Right. Duncan took me on. He and his partner Mandy started the company a few years ago. I wasn't part of the initial team, I came on about a year ago."

"And you enjoy it?"

His eyes lit up, and she knew the answer before he spoke. "Yeah. It's great being a part of a team again. When I lost my hearing, I figured it would all be over for the action and adventure stuff, but now I can still do it, thanks to Soldiering On."

Jessica grinned, his enthusiasm infectious. "That's great." She wanted to ask more about it from a business side. It sounded like a partial charity, which fascinated her, considering her own calling. But she didn't know how to ask about that without sounding like she was calling him a charity case—which he clearly wasn't—so instead she simply said, "They sound like great bosses."

"They are. I think you'd like Mandy. The two of you are similar."

Jessica filed that away later, wondering at the warmth with which Mike spoke of this Mandy woman. Was it platonic affection? Or something more?

She shook off the speculation.

"So, Soldiering On sent you to rescue me, right? You said it was because you were the only one with experience at treejumping. What the hell is that?"

He grinned and pointed up. "Parachuting into trees, and then lowering yourself down with a rope attached to the parachute."

Jessica followed his finger up. "Wait. You parachuted out of a plane, into the trees, managed not to get impaled or knocked out by something, then abseiled to the ground from all the way up there?" Incredulity made her eyes widen.

"Yeah. It's kind of dangerous. Since I was a paratrooper, I trained for this. But none of the other guys had. That's why this gig fell to me."

"You didn't want to do it?" she asked, confused by his wording. It was like he'd been forced to rescue her, not volunteered.

He grinned. "Oh, I wanted it," he said, and Jessica was pleased he wasn't here unwillingly. "I hadn't done a jump in forever. And I'm always up for a mission."

Maybe Mike was a bit of an adrenaline junky. She pressed her lips together, hoping that wouldn't mean he'd take unnecessary risks with her. Whatever he did in his own time was none of her business, but she refused to get killed because this man wanted a rush.

Though surely her parents wouldn't send someone who'd risk her life, since they'd gone to the effort of sending someone at all.

His eyes narrowed, still fixated on her lips, and Jessica made a conscious effort to smooth out her features. She didn't know what her expression had shown that annoyed him so much, but she suspected it was disapproval. She had a tendency to show her emotions, much to her politician mother's disappointment. That little flaw was enough for them both to know Jessica could never follow in Senator Vanderslice's footsteps.

"Thank you for rescuing me," she said, smoothing over the moment of awkwardness.

He nodded. "You're welcome." He took a large bite of papaya and chewed.

"After a week, I figured that no one would come. That my parents had refused to pay the ransom, and the rebels had no more use for me."

His expression darkened again. "They were stalling, giving us time to get you out."

Jessica was reluctantly touched by the fact that her parents hadn't left her to die for her mother's political ambition. She'd doubted her mother would ever pay the ransom, since it would be like admitting she negotiated with the bad guys. And her tough reputation wouldn't survive the public's shock. To Senator Vanderslice, public image was everything.

Her mother wouldn't have finagled US troops in, either, or convinced the military to launch a rescue mission. She wouldn't risk creating an international incident with Zolego, or the UN.

It hadn't occurred to Jessica that her mother might handle her kidnapping privately, instead. She hadn't even known there were companies that did things like this, but she shouldn't have been surprised.

Jessica had no doubt all the employees at Soldiering On Security had been made to sign Non-Disclosure Agreements about the whole incident, ensuring they couldn't mention their role in the rescue. It was a good sign that the company wasn't fame-hungry, since they'd get no publicity out of this. And if they'd failed to get her out of the country safely, her mother could deny all knowledge of the entire affair, since no one knew about the rescue mission. It gave her plausible deniability, which was something the senator was incredibly fond of.

"Well, thank you all the same. It can't have been easy. And that's just dealing with my mother."

Mike's eyebrows shot up. "I only met her briefly, but she seemed okay."

Jessica scoffed. "Of course she *seemed* okay. She's a career politician. She can work a room with the best of them."

"You don't get along, huh?"

Jessica sighed. "Let's say we have our differences."

He hesitated for a moment. "For what it's worth, she was really worried about you."

Jessica's heart lurched at the words. It had been a long time since she'd believed her mother cared much about her. But that didn't stop her from childishly, desperately, wanting her mother's affection and attention.

But she couldn't rely on that. Her mother wasn't one to show concern. Jessica was fairly certain the senator didn't truly care about anything other than her career, and she wasn't willing to become the desperate, hoping child again who kept getting her heart broken.

She chewed on the last of her papaya and threw away the skin.

Mike was messier than her. Clearly, he hadn't grown up learning to eat at foreign diplomats' tables as she had. She almost asked about his childhood, but then Mike produced a bottle of water from his pack and held it out to her. She drank deep, then used a tiny trickle to wet her hands, wiping away the sticky juice on her pants.

She wished she could wipe away the mud so easily—it was horribly uncomfortable on her skin now—but she knew it was better to wait until tonight, when they were flying back to the US.

Mike also cleaned his hands, then announced, "I'll check you for chigoes."

Before she even knew what was happening, he'd stepped behind her and raised her shirt, exposing her bare back to the air—and his gaze.

She squirmed and twisted out of his grip, facing him in growing outrage.

"What the hell do you think you're doing?"

He gave her an exasperated look. "Checking you for chigoes," he repeated.

"For *what?*"

"Chigoes. The fleas that burrow under your skin and lay eggs and infest you."

Jessica's stomach roiled, seconds away from losing all the papaya she'd eaten. "Even if that *is* a real thing, you can't manhandle me without my permission. Explain first."

His jaw ticked. "They are a real thing. And they can be dangerous. In case you've forgotten, we are being hunted right now, by men with guns. I don't have time to coddle you. I need you to do what I say, when I say it."

She crossed her arms over her chest. Clearly, this man did not spend any time with civilians. "That may be so, but I'm not under your command. I'm a woman who doesn't like strange men touching her without permission. It would have taken you less time to explain about chigoes and asked to touch me than it would to have this argument."

"Fine. I'm sorry. I figured you already knew about them because you've been in the country for a while. I was saving time, but in future, I'll ask." He paused. "*Unless* you are in imminent danger. I won't ask before saving your life."

She rolled her eyes. "And I wouldn't ask you to. But I'm hardly in imminent danger from a flea."

"How do I know you haven't had one buried under your skin for a week?" Mike asked. "You could very well be in danger of losing a limb at the very least."

"Is everything in this rainforest trying to kill me?" she lamented.

"It's probably safer to think like that. Rainforests are both the best and worst places to be stranded. Plenty of food and water, yes, but also plenty of deadly creatures and plants that can make you sick enough to die."

"I'm so glad I'm going home," she exhaled gustily.

"Yeah, rainforests aren't my favorite. Chigoes are sneaky little things, and they are native to this area. So, unless you want to risk infection, I'll check you all over, and then ask you to do the same for me. Okay?"

Jessica stared at him for a long moment, but his expression gave no hint he was pranking her or inventing an excuse to see her naked. In fact, he looked bored and disinterested at the possibility. And it was that which convinced her.

"I'll check you first," she said. That way, if it was all a come-on, he'd have to go through the humiliation first.

He shrugged. "Fine."

He grabbed the base of his loose, long-sleeved shirt and pulled it over his head, revealing his chest. And what a chest it was. Broad shoulders tapered down to a narrow waist. Large pecs and a flat stomach, both covered with a light dusting of hair.

She'd always been a chest woman, and this wasn't changing her mind in the slightest.

She licked her lips and reached for his water bottle again to moisten her dry mouth.

Who knew men actually looked like that outside the covers of romance novels? The men she spent the most time with were either rich charity types who didn't value muscles, or the people she volunteered with, who couldn't afford the bulk.

But this was something else. Mike's body was clearly a tool for his profession. He needed to keep it in good shape so he could jump out of planes, rescue women, and then hike through jungles without breaking a sweat. Though, that was metaphorical. Because there was a light sheen across his skin, most likely caused by the humid heat.

"Come on," he said impatiently, and Jessica shook herself out of her trance-like state. She met his gaze, only to see a hint of amusement along with his impatience.

Jessica rolled her eyes at herself. She supposed she deserved him laughing at her. She hadn't managed to hide her interest in his body at all. Well, she'd have to claw back some dignity.

She straightened her spine. "What do these chigoes look like?"

He described them in enough detail for Jessica's stomach to churn again. But she gamely stepped forward and peered closely at his chest. No hardship. Even up close, it was a thing of beauty.

She didn't see anything like what he'd described on his chest or arms. He turned at her instruction, giving her a view of his solid back. That, too, was pristine. Her hand drew towards his spine like a magnet, completely against her will. Jessica snatched her hand back before she touched him, face flaming.

When he turned back around, she raised an eyebrow. "Pants?"

He gave her another amused look. "You're not going to buy me dinner first?"

"You bought *me* dinner," she said, indicating the remains of the papaya.

"So I did."

He unbuttoned his camo pants, and Jessica watched shamelessly.

She was enjoying herself now. This moment was fun, flirtatious, a million miles away from her kidnapping and the people chasing her. She was under no illusions that the rebels would let her go without a fight. She was worth too much to them, and they wouldn't get another chance like this again since few wealthy American heiresses wandered into their country.

So she let herself enjoy this playful moment with an attractive man.

When his pants were off, revealing black boxer briefs, she crouched down to examine his legs. When she glanced up, their eyes met, and Jessica was struck by the intimacy of their position. She cleared her throat as heat bloomed across her cheeks. A light flirtation was one thing. But kneeling in front of a mostly-naked man with his junk in her face was a bit more than she'd bargained for.

Hopefully he wouldn't get any ideas.

Hell, hopefully, *she* wouldn't get any ideas.

She finished the rest of her examination as quickly as possible, then stood.

"All clear," she told him, not quite meeting his gaze. "Other than the bits I didn't see." She waved her hand near his boxer briefs.

He nodded and donned his clothes again. "Your turn."

Jessica swallowed, but she reluctantly unbuttoned her shirt and pulled off her tank top. She expected Mike to make some crass remark, or at least leer. But he didn't do anything to make her uncomfortable. He examined her as perfunctorily as a doctor would, even when she lowered her pants.

He barely noticed she was a woman, as far as she could tell, and Jessica was absurdly grateful he didn't take advantage of the situation. She might find him attractive, but she was at his mercy out here. And she had no intention of acting on said attraction, anyway.

He finished, announcing she was clear, and then stepped away, turning his back as she got dressed again. When she was ready, she tapped him on the shoulder. He spun around and gave her a cursory once-over, then nodded in satisfaction.

"We should do that every few hours, but I don't think we'll need to again before we fly out this afternoon."

Jessica blew out a breath of relief. Not that she hated staring at Mike's naked form. But it was embarrassing to be mutually semi-naked with a man you had no intention of sleeping with. Even now, a strange wall lay between them, which they'd both erected to keep the boundaries in place.

Just as well. He was presumptuous, and a little rude. She didn't need to make friends with him, or lust after him, or anything other than rely on him to get her home safe.

And once she was home, she wouldn't ever see him again.

CHAPTER FOUR

They reached the airport at fifteen hundred hours. Perfect timing.

Mike had kept their food and water breaks to a minimum. He hadn't needed the rest, but Jessica had struggled. Sweat dampened every inch of her, sticking her clothes to her skin. She kept stumbling, whether from lack of food, injury, or an unfamiliarity with the terrain, he didn't know. But he'd pushed her anyway, even if guilt nagged at him.

It was best to get her out of the country as soon as possible. One day of discomfort wouldn't matter much in the scheme of things. And she had put on a brave face, a fact he admired.

When he'd been told he had to rescue a senator's daughter—a Vanderslice at that—he'd expected a spoiled, difficult woman. Instead, she hadn't complained once, even as he'd pushed her to her limits. And this was after she'd already spent a week in captivity, where God knew what had happened to her.

He should have known she wasn't the high-maintenance type. After all, she'd been doing charity work in countries like this for years. Her mother had announced this proudly when Mike had questioned why she was in Zolego in the first place. Jessica would be used to harder labor than the average senator's daughter.

Jessica crept closer to the lush ferns they hid behind. He tore his eyes from her and followed her gaze to the airport beyond. Though calling it an airport was a bit of a stretch.

Really, it was a short landing strip carved out of the encroaching jungle. It wasn't well-maintained. The greenery pushed in on all sides and littered the runway, such as it was, with vines and sticks and leaves.

It was lucky Charlie was such a good pilot, or he'd have difficulty landing the POS plane he'd rented for them.

What passed for a control tower stood at the end of the runway, about forty feet from where Mike and Jessica crouched. A staircase ran the side of the hut, leading to a room about one and a half stories above the ground. It didn't even come close to reaching the height of the trees surrounding it, so Mike wasn't sure why they'd bothered. Surely it wouldn't have helped them see incoming planes any better. It looked about three seconds away from falling over, the bamboo and other wood sagging under the weight of whoever was inside. It swayed lightly, too, making Mike think the people were moving around.

The control tower was only big enough for about four people to sit uncomfortably, so there couldn't be many of them. These guys must have been the ones Charlie had made the deal with to be allowed to land. He hoped they were as good as their word.

Charlie would arrive at any moment.

Something nudged his shoulder and Mike glanced over to see Jessica's expectant face.

"Well?" she asked.

"Well, what?"

"What's next?"

"We wait," he said simply. "Charlie is due within the hour. I don't want to head to the tower and press our luck with whoever is in there. I don't know exactly what Charlie promised them, but he did say they were hesitant to help an American."

"No surprise," she said. "This is rebel territory. If they knew what he was flying in for, they wouldn't be happy."

A cold chill crept over the back of Mike's neck, a hint of foreboding despite the oppressive heat beneath the trees. It was an intuition he always listened to. He wasn't sure whether to hope Charlie had warned these guys about Jessica or not.

Hopefully they'd get away with bringing her here, or at least have a chance to negotiate with these rebels, or bribe them. Whatever it took to get Jessica home safely.

"When Charlie comes, he'll take us across the border into Colombia," Mike told Jessica. "From there, he'll return the plane, while the two of us will charter a jet to take us back stateside."

She nodded. "A shower first, though, I hope," she said.

"Hmmm," Mike answered, mind immediately landing on an image of Jessica in the shower. Naked. Water sliding over that perfect skin. His blood rushed south.

She plucked at the tank top hewing to her skin. The movement drew Mike's eyes, landing on the gaping top where a hint of her breasts were visible.

He'd already seen those in more detail, though her sensible sports bra had hidden most of her assets. That hadn't stopped Mike from paying attention, no matter how much he tried not to.

Her figure was slim, like a runner, but with naturally ample breasts. She was fairly tall, though still a head shorter than his own six foot four. She was strong, too, with more defined muscles than he'd expected. It was clear she worked to keep herself in good shape, another fact that shouldn't have surprised him. Her delicate facial features belied the strength in her body and her soul.

He swore to himself that he'd been genuinely checking for chigoes earlier, not faking an excuse to see Jessica mostly naked. But he was a red-blooded man who appreciated a stunning woman when he saw one. It was primal, and irresistible. He was also an excellent poker player, so she never needed to know he'd struggled to keep his eyes off her curves.

"I wouldn't mind a shower myself," he murmured. A cold one that would help get this ridiculous lust under control. He was a grown man for fuck's sake. And he shouldn't be fantasizing over her like the grossest virgin teen, no matter how attractive she was.

Besides, of all the women to lust after, this was the wrong one. It was clear she came from a long line of people who worked no hard labor. Her skin was too smooth, not tanned and work-roughened like his. They were from two very different worlds.

A hand waved in front of his face, and Mike blinked back to reality. Had he been staring at her breasts? He glanced up with some trepidation to meet her annoyed gaze, one eyebrow raised in a way that told him she knew exactly where his mind had gone. Shit. Busted.

He gave her an unrepentant grin. "Sorry," he told her, knowing he probably didn't sound sorry at all. But he was. Kinda.

She rolled her eyes. "Keep your eyes to yourself. You staring is bad enough, but it's worse because you can't listen to what I'm saying when you do."

Heat flooded his cheeks, and he was suddenly grateful for the layer of thick mud over his face so she didn't see. She was right. Staring at her like she was an object was bad enough. But to do so in a way that meant he couldn't read her lips was so much worse, like he was reducing her to an object without a voice.

"Sorry," he said again, this time more sincerely.

She nodded, her face smoothing of its annoyance. "For what it's worth, I am sorry about the distraction. I seriously can't wait to have a shower and get some clean clothes."

Had the rebels let her bathe when they'd held her captive? He opened his mouth to ask, but her gaze snapped to something over his shoulder. He turned, expecting the rebels, but instead it was a small plane in the distance.

Mike checked his watch. Sure enough, Charlie was right on time.

He stood, preparing to run for the plane when it landed. But movement near the tower caught his attention. Three men stumbled out of the room and boosted each other onto the roof of the tower.

Mike had a brief moment of confusion—would they signal Charlie in?—when he saw it.

A gun.

And not just any gun, but a machine gun, mounted to the roof.

One of the men hauled the barrel until it pointed in Charlie's direction.

Mike ran before conscious thought even penetrated, heart racing with fear. He couldn't let them shoot Charlie out of the sky. And he had no way of warning Charlie what was about to happen.

Shit, why had he believed they'd let him land and take Jessica out of the country? She was their meal ticket to a better life. He'd trusted Charlie had known what he was doing, as he would every member of Duncan's team, but the guy had royally screwed up if they were seconds away from machine gunning his plane into the jungle.

Mike reached the base of the stairs as gunfire flashed above him.

He sprinted up the steps three at a time, ignoring the way the structure swayed under his determined movements. If the whole thing collapsed, at least they'd have to stop shooting.

When he got to the top, Mike raised the semi-automatic he'd stolen from one of the rebels back at camp. They likely hadn't heard him over the rattle of the machine gun, a sound he remembered well enough.

He squeezed the trigger. One of the three rebels dropped, the one who had been standing closest to the edge of the roof. He toppled over and landed hard on the landing next to Mike. The wood collapsed slightly under the weight, and it shifted alarmingly beneath Mike's boots.

The rebel's companion—the one feeding the machine gun—spun around in shock. His eyes widened as he caught sight of Mike.

He opened his mouth to warn the third man, but Mike dropped him with a bullet to the head before he could say anything. He fell backward, disappearing out of sight, likely landing on the ground below.

That left rebel number three. Adrenaline surged through Mike's system. Due to the angle of the roof and where he stood, Mike couldn't actually see the final man. He'd have to get on that roof if he wanted to take him out.

Thankfully, Charlie's plane was still in the sky, circling beyond the machine gun's range. There wasn't any damage to the hull, and Mike grinned. Charlie sure was a lucky son of a bitch, and a hell of a flier. Under his touch, the plane was a lot more nimble than the cumbersome machine gun still spewing bullet its way.

Mike eyed the distance to the roof. He could grab it, no problem. But he'd be vulnerable to any attack as he pulled himself up, since he couldn't keep his weapon trained on the shooter while hauling himself up two-handed.

Shit.

The railing around the landing didn't look like it would hold Mike's weight, but he didn't have much choice. It would at least give him enough extra height to get eyes on the shooter.

He stepped over the body of the dead man and pushed his foot against the railing. It gave, but it didn't crack. It would have to do.

With his left hand, he grabbed the lip of the roof. With his right, he kept a strong grip on the gun. Then, he planted his foot and pulled himself up as softly as he could. The rail held, and raised him enough to see the machine gun operator, who still had his back to Mike.

Mike leaned against the wall for balance and put his left hand on the gun, steadying his aim. He released a breath and pulled the trigger, long enough for a burst of bullets to escape the gun and bury deep into the shooter's back. The man slumped forward over the weapon and immediately went still.

Mike breathed a sigh of relief, but his blood still ran hot from the firefight. Gingerly, he stepped down from the rickety rail. The landing wasn't much stronger, but he it held his weight better.

He peeked into the room the men had come from. No more rebels. The tiny space only held three chairs and a table. On the table sat a two-way radio and an abandoned game of cards.

Now that the threat had been eliminated, he turned back to the stairs, intending to collect Jessica from the rainforest where he'd left her.

Instead, he found her waiting at the bottom of the staircase. He scowled at her. Why the hell had she run towards danger? Her mouth moved, but she was too far for him to read her lips accurately.

He waved her up, and she trotted up the steps immediately, her steps far softer than his since they didn't sway the structure.

"What the hell are you doing?" he growled.

"I thought I could help," she replied.

"In a firefight?" he replied skeptically.

She shrugged. "It's possible. I was hardly going to be left behind while you went into battle for me." He eyes strayed to the dead man on the landing. "Though did you really have to kill them?"

His mouth pressed into a thin line. "Since it was a choice between them and my friend? Yes."

She narrowed her gaze but didn't contradict him. Her eyes, however, told him she was sad for the men who had seconds ago been shooting at one of her rescuers. Where did this woman's loyalty lie? And why was she so sympathetic to the group that had kidnapped her and held her hostage for a full week?

A terrible suspicion wormed its way into his brain. Surely she hadn't staged her own kidnapping to extort money from her parents? Maybe she was in deep with the rebels, and wanted to support their cause financially, but hadn't had the money to do so. Or maybe she hadn't wanted to spend her own money and had figured her parents had deeper pockets.

If the kidnapping was staged, why had she been tied up when he'd arrived? Surely they wouldn't have known he was coming. Or maybe they had. Maybe he'd messed up, and made more noise than he'd thought. Or maybe she'd suspected her parents would send someone instead of paying the ransom, and she hadn't wanted to take any chances and give the game away.

Or maybe there were spies in the capital who had told the rebels of Mike and Charlie's arrival. These days there weren't too many visitors to Zolego, given the political instability of the country. Two American men—clearly military—would have stood out in the small capital city.

He eyed Jessica. He didn't want to believe she'd trick her parents like that. But she'd hinted earlier they weren't close. Maybe this was even some kind of twisted revenge scheme?

"How were you kidnapped?" Mike asked.

She blinked at him, clearly surprised by his question. "You don't know?"

He shook his head. "The ransom video the rebels sent didn't give specifics, only that they had you."

"What does it have to do with anything?"

"Just humor me."

"They took me from the orphanage where I volunteer with the children. I teach English there. One day, about twenty rebels burst in and demanded I go with them. I refused. They put a gun to the heads of some of the children in my class and said if I didn't go with them, they'd kill the children. I couldn't allow that, so I went."

The mix of detachment in her words and the tears in her eyes made Mike inclined to believe her story. He'd seen enough trauma survivors to know the signs. Distancing themselves emotionally from the event while still relieving its every moment. If she was really faking it, she was an Oscar-worthy actress.

But still. She was awfully fond of these rebels for a woman who had supposedly experienced a nightmare at their hands.

"And then what happened?" he asked.

"They took me to somewhere on the outskirts of the city. Held me in a house while they recorded the ransom video. The next day, they drove into the rainforest until there was no more road. We hiked for a day before we reached the camp where you found me."

He continued to stare at her, parsing through her words to discover the lie. But he couldn't find it. The scenario sounded plausible. Her recounting of the rebels putting a gun to the heads of children made his teeth clench in anger, but she didn't seem to harbor the same resentment.

"And yet you still don't want the rebels to die, even though they did all this to you."

She sucked in a deep breath and straightened her spine. "That's right. I don't blame desperate people for doing desperate things. They need money to overthrow the government and save their people. I was one of the few ways they could get it. I understand, even if I hate that it was me they chose."

"Doing bad things for a good cause is still doing a bad thing. If the rebels continue down this path, they'll be no better than the asshole they are trying to depose."

"You're right," she said. "And I don't condone what they did. I hope they never do it again. But I understand why they did it, why they felt like they had no other choice." She hesitated. "I don't want any more people killed."

He let out a long breath. "Fine. Doesn't matter, anyway. We're out of here."

He turned and strode into the room, towards the radio. It wasn't the time or the place to debate politics with a woman like her. It wasn't ever the time. She clearly had a different view of the world than he did, most likely because she'd grown up with a life of privilege as a politician's daughter. Had she witnessed her mother do bad things for a good cause? Had it impacted her in ways she wasn't really aware of? He couldn't be sure.

That was if she wasn't secretly working with the rebels for her own reasons. He wasn't convinced she was entirely innocent of that.

Mike pushed the thought out of his mind and flicked the radio dials until he reached the wavelength Charlie should be operating under. Then, he waved Jessica over and shoved the received at her.

"This should be Charlie. You'll have to talk to him. Let him know it's safe to land." He showed her how to use the device, annoyed he couldn't do it himself. But without lip reading or his voice-to-text machine, he was useless in situations like this.

"Hello, is that Charlie?" Jessica asked into the radio. After a moment, her face cleared. "Yes, Mike says it's safe to land…Yes, see you soon."

Jessica turned to him with a smile. "He's coming in now."

Ah shit. Surely a woman with a smile like that wouldn't be devious enough to extort money from her own parents. It was too pure, too real.

Or maybe that was his dick talking because he found her attractive. He didn't want to have come all this way to rescue a woman who didn't need rescuing. He wanted to believe she was exactly as she seemed—a rich woman with a big heart, who saw the best in everybody. But Mike had lived a cynical life, and it had served him well so far. Few people had pleasantly surprised him in his years on this planet. Many had lived down to his low expectations.

But this woman made him want to believe.

He turned away from her in disgust at himself. He didn't know this woman. She could be the worst humanity had to offer for all he knew. Didn't matter if she was brave and kind and strong.

Though he couldn't quite seem to convince himself of that.

Outside the window, movement flickered at the edge of the trees. He couldn't see what it was. A panther? Or was that…?

Oh, shit.

He spun around. "Call Charlie back, tell him not to land." Urgency thrummed through him. From the air, Charlie wouldn't see the men surrounding them. He'd be a sitting duck as soon as he got into range.

"What? Why?"

"The rebels. They're here. Quickly!" He pushed her lightly in the direction of the radio. She picked up the receiver and spoke into it. He couldn't see her lips move—her back was to him—but he glanced out the window in time to see Charlie veering away.

"Tell him we'll meet him across the border in Colombia. He'll have to wait for us. I don't want him to try landing in Zolego again."

Jessica nodded and then relayed that to Charlie. Tension lined her frame, and even without his hearing, he knew her voice would be taut and urgent.

The rebels were closing in. As soon as the plane turned around, they'd come out of hiding, moving in the direction of the tower. The men were in the open, sitting ducks.

"I'm going to shoot these guys," he announced. Damned if he'd let them take Jessica again. No matter who or what she might be, he was hired to do a job, and he intended to do it. His mission was to get Jessica out of the country by any means necessary, and that's what he intended to do, regardless of her bleeding heart.

He didn't turn to see if Jessica said anything to stop him, so he stuck the gun out of the open window and pulled the trigger. He laid down fire, not aiming at the rebels in spite of himself. Jessica must be rubbing off on him.

"Head for the trees," he called to her as the rebels scattered back. He'd provide cover fire while she escaped, then head after her.

But instead of obeying him, she appeared at his elbow. He glanced her way, frowning. Why wasn't she following orders?

"They won't hurt me," she declared, tugging on his arm. "They need me alive."

"You can't be sure of that."

"Maybe not certain, but it's a good bet. There's no reason for them to come after me if they don't want me as a hostage. They must want me returned to them, or they wouldn't have bothered chasing us."

"So, you want to go back to them?" he asked incredulously.

She shook her head. "Stay behind me and they won't shoot."

He stared at her in horror. There was no way he'd let her protect him. It was *his* job to protect *her* for fuck's sake.

"You don't know that and I'm not taking the chance. Get to the trees."

"Not without you."

Her jaw was set in a stubborn line. There was no way he'd convince her to see reason. Not in the limited time he had.

She tugged on his arm again, and this time he followed her to the door. Below, a group of men in ragged clothes waited for them, guns ready. Mike raised his weapon, ready to fire. But then Jessica stepped in front of him with her arms up, a gesture of surrender. The damned woman wouldn't be reasonable.

The rebels hesitated for a split second, giving Mike enough time to pull the trigger. The men dove for cover, away from his haphazard bullets. One caught a man in the shoulder and he went down, clutching at the wound.

Jessica turned an outraged glare on him, but he ignored her, shoving her towards the stairs. She stumbled, then righted herself, running down the steps as he followed. He shot in the direction of anyone who got too close, keeping them all at a distance. They were all reluctant to fire, with Jessica so close. She was clearly right that they wanted her alive.

But it was inevitable that some brave soul would shoot at them regardless. The air moved as a bullet whipped past his head. Mike ducked but kept moving. He glanced in the direction the shooter must be, in time to see a young guy with shaking hands, panic written across his features.

It was never clearer to Mike that these rebels were untrained. This guy was a kid, and one who had no idea how to hold a weapon.

Guilt burrowed into him. It was almost cruel for a man like himself to go against inexperienced kids. He'd had a decade in the military, and some of the most rigorous training known to man. Even with their numbers, it wasn't a fair fight.

Maybe what Jessica said had some truth to it.

But he couldn't think about that now. Not when these rebels—inexperienced or no—might shoot both Mike and the woman he was here to protect.

He raised his gun and fired at their feet, aiming precisely so it looked like he was attempting to hit them. It worked. They stumbled away from him.

A man about two decades older than Mike stood up in a Jeep beyond the main clutch of rebels, the same one Mike had seen at the compound. He was definitely the leader of the ragtag group, since he wore an actual uniform. Mike didn't know what the unfamiliar patches and symbols on his jacket meant, but they seemed impressive. This man's bearing clearly indicated he'd been properly trained, as Mike had been.

The leader of the rebels? Maybe. He certainly looked dignified enough. And the determined fury on his face made Mike's stomach tighten. This guy was dangerous, no question.

But that didn't matter now. Not when he needed to get Jessica to safety.

Mike fired again, driving the rebels back from the path to the forest. Many of them were so distracted dodging the bullets coming their way they lowered their guns. Mike took full advantage, pushing Jessica between the trees. He backed in behind her, keeping his eyes on the rebels and his gun trained on them, daring them to make a move. But they didn't. They only watched him and Jessica go with desperation in their eyes.

Once they were out of sight, Mike turned and ran, dragging Jessica behind him.

Well, this had turned into quite a clusterfuck.

CHAPTER FIVE

"How long to the border?" Jessica asked and took a sip of water.

"A week, give or take," Mike said with a shrug.

Jessica choked on the water she'd swallowed. "*A week?*" Her voice came out at a screech, and for once she was glad Mike was deaf so he couldn't hear the unflattering sound.

He nodded. "It's not ideal. We'll have to rethink our strategy."

Jessica stared at him in the darkening twilight. They'd stopped for a drink a few minutes ago, finally giving Jessica a chance to catch her breath. Now, though, the oppressive air of the rainforest was like a vice on her lungs, squeezing it so tight she could barely breathe.

She'd been so looking forward to being home. A shower. Safety. Tears sprang to her eyes at the knowledge she'd have to wait another full week for all those things.

"Will we be in the jungle the whole time?" she asked in a small voice.

"Well, we're in the middle of the Amazon. It's not like there are many cities between us and the border."

"So, it'll just be us…in *this*?" Jessica knew she sounded ungrateful, but Jesus this isn't what she'd wanted. She'd managed to hold it together this far, but panic and desperation were setting in. She didn't know if she was strong enough to do this.

"Probably safest," Mike answered. "We have no idea who to trust. If someone tells the rebels where we are, they'll come after us. And I think they'll be better prepared next time."

"How did they find us?" she asked. Surely they'd moved fast enough that the rebels would have struggled to catch up with them. She'd barely kept up, and she was decently fit. Nothing like Mike, of course, with his insane body and endless stamina. But the rebels would have been closer to her level than Mike's inhuman abilities.

"They had transport," he said. "At least one car. They must have figured out our destination and grabbed the Jeeps, gone around the long way."

She hadn't considered that. "Oh crap. Do you think that will happen again?"

"They'll meet us at the border, you mean? I doubt it. That's a long stretch of land, and the rebels have no way of knowing where we'll come out. I think if they want to catch us, they'd be better off tracking us."

"But you're not sure?"

"No," he replied, jaw tense. Clearly, he didn't like not having the answers. "So we'll have to be prepared for an attack from ahead or behind."

Jessica let out a long breath. "A week," she murmured in a small voice. The tears she'd fought off moments ago came back with a vengeance, and this time she couldn't blink them away. They slipped down her cheeks as she thought about the long, difficult hike ahead of her. She wanted to be home, dammit.

There was a light touch on her arm, almost hesitant. Jessica didn't even think. She tipped forward with her eyes closed until her forehead landed on Mike's chest. She let out a sob, and his arms came around her.

Under normal circumstances, a man like Mike would not be her first choice for comfort as she cried. In fact, he'd probably be the last. But since he was the only other person for miles around that didn't want to kidnap or hurt her, she took what she could get as she wept into his hard chest.

To her surprise, he wasn't terrible at comforting her. His arms were strong and warm as they wrapped around her, his hands firm as he rubbed her back. He didn't berate her for being weak, or tell her to suck it up and get over it as she might have expected.

Instead, he murmured soothing nonsense sounds, the noise as comforting as the deep vibration coming from his chest as he did so.

So Jessica let herself feel. The hopelessness, the regret, the frustration, the anger. All the emotions that had been building in her, that she'd put off when she thought she'd be home soon, intending to deal with them later.

It wasn't only today, or the long journey ahead of them. It was the last week, since the rebels had burst into the orphanage and threatened her and those children. Nothing had gone right for her since that moment.

It had been an insanely difficult time, and her nerves had been stretched thin. The ticket home had been *so close* before it had been snatched away again. She'd wanted to cry as she'd told Charlie to turn back, to meet them over the border. She'd held on thinking it couldn't be too far away, but she'd been wrong. So wrong.

"A week," she sobbed, but of course Mike didn't reply.

She took a deep breath. Okay, a week. It wasn't so terrible in the grand scheme of things. They only had to survive a week in the jungle with no supplies and they'd be fine. Piece of cake.

As much as the idea panicked Jessica, Mike wasn't freaking out. So he mustn't be concerned they'd die out here. He must have a plan.

She took comfort in that strength, drawing it into her. They'd be fine. The news was a shock, is all.

Jessica sucked in another breath, and another, until she steadied. Then, she slowly eased herself away from Mike's chest. She was surprisingly reluctant to go, finding she'd be happy spending a lot more time in his arms, against those hard muscles. And from the slow way he released her, perhaps he felt the same.

Mud was smeared where she'd pressed her face against him. She'd forgotten about the stupid mask on her face.

She glanced up to apologize, only to be frozen by the expression on his face. It was a kind of tenderness that was wholly unexpected. Maybe it was a trick of the rapidly fading light. She shook herself. What had she been saying?

"Are you okay?" Mike asked on a rumble.

She nodded. "I'm sorry about that. It's out of my system now."

He smiled. "It's okay. I'm upset, too. This wasn't how I planned this mission to go."

"You don't *look* very upset," she said doubtfully.

"I'm crying on the inside," he said with a wink. She laughed, as he'd no doubt meant her to.

Then, he pulled out his flashlight and clicked it on. She sighed.

"We have to keep going?" she asked.

"Just a little farther. I need to find a good place to stop." He checked the clip on the automatic rifles they'd been carrying, then threw them to the side. They must be empty.

Jessica was ready to sleep right here. Every part of her ached. She'd been walking all day, she was soaked in sweat, and she was sure her feet were blistered. But instead of saying any of that, instead of crying again, she straightened her spine and nodded.

They headed off, Jessica following the flashlight through the darkness. It could only have been thirty minutes when Mike stopped again.

"Here?" Jessica asked when he turned to her.

"Here," he confirmed.

She sank to the soft forest floor in relief. "Thank God."

"You, uh, might not want to stay down there. The insects, you know."

Jessica immediately scrambled to her feet. "What? Are you kidding?" She searched the ground in the pale light of the flashlight but couldn't see any creepy crawlies.

"Not kidding," Mike said. "I'll have to make us some hammocks to sleep on, to avoid them. The chigoes alone live a few inches beneath the surface, and they'd love to latch onto you. We're also close enough to water that you might get some leeches."

Jessica swallowed, scared she might faint. *Leeches?* No, thank you.

Mike set down his pack. "Sit on that for now. I'll make camp."

"I'll help," Jessica declared, not willing to get too close to the ground.

Mike bent down and grabbed a metal pot from his pack. "There's a stream down there," he said, pointing with the flashlight. She could see a trickle of water at the edge of the beam. "Fill this with water, but don't drink it. We'll need to boil it first."

Jessica nodded and did as he instructed. As much as the water tempted her, she trusted Mike's advice and didn't drink it. She did, however, wash the mud from her face and hands. If it had been deep enough, she would have stripped down and dived in, Mike be damned, but the stream barely covered the pot.

She did strip off her outer shirt and sluice water over her arms and underarms. Washing off the sweat made her feel slightly more human, but it wasn't perfect. She'd never take a shower for granted ever again.

By the time she returned to Mike, he had a small fire crackling merrily and a collection of various plants waiting nearby.

"Won't they see the fire?" she asked.

He shrugged. "Maybe, but I think the undergrowth is dense enough to hide it unless they're right on top of us."

He took the water from her and hung it over the fire using sticks he'd propped into a frame. Then, he wrapped the various vegetables in some kind of large leaf and dug them into the embers of the fire. When that was done, he stood.

"I need to get some stuff for the hammocks. Don't go anywhere."

Like she had any intention of wandering off into the darkness. But she didn't say that to him, simply nodded and watched as he strode around at the edge of the fire's light.

"Aha," he said eventually, and came back with a couple of young bamboo shoots even taller than he was.

"You're making a hammock out of bamboo?" she asked. "I didn't even know bamboo grew here."

"It's native to the far east, but it's spread everywhere tropical. I was surprised to find some this deep in the rainforest, though."

She nodded. "So how do you make a hammock out of that?"

"Let me show you," he said with a grin. He dug a piece of oiled fabric from his pack—a raincoat?—and laid it out. "You'll have to sit next to me. I've only got one of these."

He sat, and Jessica moved hesitantly over and lowered herself beside him. Her butt barely fit on the fabric. She had to press herself to his side, so close she could feel every hard inch of him.

He seemed wholly unaffected by her presence, so she did her best to ignore the heat radiating from him. Instead, she watched as he cut slices in one of the bamboo shoots, about a foot from each end. He used a shorter knife than the kukri blade, much more convenient for the small work. How many weapons did he carry on him?

She was almost afraid to ask.

He sliced longways on the bamboo, from the point of his previous cut to the other, until he pulled off the top, leaving a canoe shape behind. He stood and pulled some vines down from the nearest tree, tying one solidly around each end of the bamboo. Then, he used the knife to cut two-inch strips in the canoe part of the bamboo. Jessica was fascinated, watching his deft hands work quickly and efficiently on the pliable wood. Then, he fanned out the strips, testing them, but they bounced back into position.

Next, he took the discarded lid of the canoe and cut it into more strips. He wove those strips through the others, fanning them out again. This time, with the other strips woven through, they stayed fanned out. Exactly in the shape of a hammock.

"Oh my goodness, that's so clever," she murmured.

"Not the most comfortable, but it'll do," he said. "Better than sleeping on the forest floor, believe me."

She thought again of the chigoes he'd described and shivered. She had no doubt he was right.

He tied up the hammock, and then made swift work of another one. "If I'd known we'd be spending the night, I might have brought some hammocks with me," he said on a sigh as he tied the second hammock between two trees on the opposite side of the fire to the first one.

"Why didn't you bring at least one anyway? In case?"

He raised an eyebrow. "I was jumping out of a plane, into the rainforest, in the dark. I didn't want my pack to be any heavier than necessary."

She exhaled. Yeah, that made sense. "Well, I'm glad you've got the skills necessary to survive out here without all the supplies."

He chuckled. "Me, too. I suppose all those years in the paratroopers paid off."

Jessica smiled. She was sure he'd done a lot of good in his time in the military. He certainly seemed like the type, who believed in doing good things for the right reasons. Perhaps that was why he was so resistant to her belief that the rebels weren't the totally evil villains he believed them to be. War had made him see in terms of good guys, and bad. In conflict, shades of gray were discouraged.

Or maybe it was just who he was. Maybe he believed in doing the right thing no matter the circumstances.

"Let's eat," he said, pulling her out of her thoughts.

Her stomach grumbled violently at his words. Christ, she was starving. The water boiled, so he took that off the fire and let it sit in the dirt beside it. He used two sticks to pinch the wrapped vegetables and pull them from the embers of the fire. On the raincoat, he carefully unwrapped one of the vegetables. It was a root of some kind.

"What is that?" she asked.

"Taro," he replied. "It's good, but it needs to be cooked. Can't be eaten raw like papaya."

She nodded. He proceeded to carefully unwrap the other vegetables, none of which she recognized. He told her the names of all of them, but she promptly forgot them at the sight of real food. She'd gnaw off her own arm if it meant filling her stomach at this point.

"Careful, it's hot," he said as he handed her the taro.

She took it from him and blew on it impatiently. Before it was ready, she took a bite. It burned her tongue, but it was so worth it. It was the best food she'd ever tasted, purely because it had been forever since she'd eaten proper food. Papaya only got a girl so far, particularly given how far they'd walked today.

She moaned in pleasure and took another bite. She never wanted to go without food again.

Once she'd finished that, Mike handed her some more. They ate side-by-side, making their way through all the vegetables he'd collected until Jessica was full. Then, he filled his canteen with the water they'd boiled earlier and offered it to her. She drank deeply, then handed it back to him.

The fire and Mike's body heat made her sticky again, but Jessica couldn't bring herself to move away. She was content and unwinding in the small, intimate pool of light. Mike's presence was a comfort, like a barrier between her and all the horrors that lay beyond the light. No rebels, or spiders, or chigoes could reach her here with Mike beside her.

And, yes, she had a long trek again tomorrow, but at least she would get home eventually. She trusted Mike would make that happen.

Full for the first time in over a week, Jessica yawned and leaned deeper into Mike's arm.

It would be okay. She had to believe that.

Mike couldn't stop watching her lips. He told himself it was purely so he'd know if she said anything, but it was a lie. Because all he could think about was kissing her.

The pleasure on her face as she ate wasn't helping. It sent his mind straight into the gutter, wondering if that would be her expression if he made love to her.

He cleared his throat and threw another piece of wood on the fire. He only had small sticks and rotted pieces of fallen trees, since he didn't have time to chop down a fresh tree. He'd need to feed it constantly to keep the fire burning through the night. They didn't need it for warmth, but it would help scare off predators, and would anchor him in the dark without his hearing.

He hadn't wanted to tell Jessica, but he was nervous about their hike through the rainforest. It was bad enough being deaf in the city, unable to hear honking horns, or calls of warning, or any other sounds that kept people safe.

But in the rainforest, with its far deadlier predators, the crack of a branch or the buzz of a mosquito might be all that stood between him and death. Or, worse, *Jessica* and death.

There would be big cats in this area, along with the chigoes, leeches, spiders, and other creepy crawlies. Any of those could cause injury or even death if they weren't careful.

And to top it all off, they had an entire rebel army hunting them, desperate for the payday they believed Jessica would bring. He could hope they'd give up, and decide it wasn't worth the effort of chasing them through the rainforest. But even out here in the middle of nowhere, the rebels must know what she was worth.

Jessica's father was from one of the wealthiest families in the country—and she was the last of its line. From his research on the plane to Zolego, Mike knew her future fortune was valued at over a billion dollars.

That kind of money was more than the entire gross domestic product of Zolego by an embarrassing amount. It was life-changing for these rebels.

Mike couldn't imagine what it would be like to grow up so rich and privileged. It was a foreign world to a man who was raised in a dying town in America's heartland. More foreign even than the warzones he'd spent so many years in.

He turned to Jessica, determined to distract himself from thoughts of his childhood.

"What was it like?" he asked.

"What?"

"Growing up like you did?"

She pursed her lips. "Cold," she said, surprising him. "The house I was raised in had a lot of marble. And my parents didn't make up for the lack of warmth."

Her expression was flat as she talked.

He frowned. "It can't have been that bad. All that money? Had to count for something."

She shrugged. "I would have given it all up for my mom to read me a bedtime story." Her chest rose and fell on a sigh.

"Jesus." At least his mom had given him that much. "So you guys don't get along?"

She shook her head. "I took my trust fund when I turned eighteen and went to see the world. I wanted to do more, see more, than the path my parents had laid out for me. Of course, I then saw the reality of the world, and the stark contrast to all my privilege shocked me. I'd never really known except in the most vague sense."

"And that's when you got into your volunteer work?"

She nodded. "My parents have all the money in the world, and what did it get us? Nothing. Coldness and misery. I wanted to use my money to bring happiness instead."

She was so matter-of-fact about it all. As if it hadn't been a huge, life-changing revelation she'd been through. As if this was something everyone experienced. Maybe in some ways they did. Hadn't he abandoned the life he'd known to experience more of the wider world? Found himself helping people? And having adventures in foreign lands?

Not the same, but he and Jessica had more in common than he'd thought.

"At least you know your parents worry about you. They sent me to save you."

She gave a bitter laugh. "Sure. Most likely because my mother has reelection coming up, and she doesn't want anything to distract voters from her campaign."

He didn't know if he could convince her otherwise. She knew her own mother better than Mike did, even though he was convinced Senator Vanderslice had been terrified for her daughter. Maybe he'd been fooled.

"I see you on the news during election time." He hadn't meant to admit that. It implied he'd noticed her, remembered her. And that was a little too close to the truth.

"I help with my mother's campaigns. We don't get along, but she's a decent politician. I'd rather she get elected than some of the assholes who have run against her. Besides, every time I'm in the news, they usually mention the charities I support. You know,"—she put on a newscaster's voice—"'Jessica

Vanderslice, who recently returned from volunteer work in Sudan…' and the charities I support get an influx of donations. I figure it can't hurt to keep my public profile up as long as that's still the case."

She sent him a self-deprecating grin, and he smiled in response. This woman was nothing like what he'd expected. Seeing her on the stage next to her mother, so cool and collected, not a hair out of place, he'd thought she'd be prissy and spoiled.

Instead, she was down to earth, with a sense of humor that was often directed at herself. She cared about others, more than she did about herself. She was brave, and strong. She'd trekked through a deadly rainforest all day with barely a word of complaint. Yes, she'd broken down briefly earlier, but it was a completely understandable—even normal—reaction. And it had given him a chance to wrap his arms around her, feel her soft body against his. He couldn't complain about that.

He liked this woman more than the cool ice-queen she presented for her mother's campaigns. She was real, and within reach. The kind of woman that he could see himself spending time with on a normal day, when not forced together by an endless rainforest surrounding them.

Not that he would. He wasn't exactly the relationship type. But still. There was something about this woman.

"What about you?" she asked, shifting to draw his attention.

He blinked. "What about me?"

"Where did you grow up? What was your family like?"

He shrugged. "I was born in this factory town in the midwest. The factories had started shutting down a few years before I was born, but my parents stubbornly stayed, even after my father lost his job. We didn't grow up with much. After I finished high school I searched for work—couldn't see myself leaving town, the only place I'd ever known—but it was impossible. There was nothing there. No jobs, no future. So I joined the military."

"How old were you?"

"Nineteen."

"And you enjoyed it?"

"Yeah. For the first time it was like I had a future in front of me, you know? All kinds of possibilities. It was a kind of adventure I'd never really dreamed of."

He sighed. Until an IED had exploded near him and taken it away again. It was like all the hopes and dreams he'd built over a decade of being a part of something were snatched away the second he was told his hearing wouldn't come back.

Until Duncan had found him and convinced him to apply for a job at Soldiering On Security, he'd really believed he was worse off even than the first time he left his hometown. This time he'd had no prospects *and* no hearing.

"And how did you end up with your current job?" she asked.

He smiled. "Duncan—my boss—has contacts with all the local VA hospitals. He asks them to give him hints if they think anyone who passes through might be a good candidate for his company."

"And they passed on your name?"

"God knows why. I was a mess. I drank a bit too heavily. I planned to go back to my hometown with my tail between my legs, but I couldn't bring myself to do it. The alcohol was for courage, I guess, and drowning my sorrows. And then Duncan knocked on my door. I thought he was kidding at first."

"But he wasn't?"

"No. He showed me all the recent news articles about the company. I hadn't heard of them, but Soldiering On Security had made a name for themselves. He invited me to apply for a position. I nearly didn't. I didn't think he'd take me. But in the end I suppose I had a bit more hope than sense, so I sent in an application. A few days later I had a job."

It had saved him, getting that job. He'd been on a downward spiral and Duncan had pulled him out before he'd got in too deep.

"Of course he did. You're perfect for this kind of thing. Look what you've achieved here," she said, waving her hand at their camp, and to the jungle beyond where they'd had their adventures earlier in the day. Warmth spread through his chest at the praise.

Rather than saying anything, he shrugged. "I was still in the adjustment period after losing my hearing.

I'd already started learning to read lips, and sign language, by that point. But I was more diligent after getting the job. Among all the other things I do, it's helpful to read lips during surveillance, and such."

"Of course."

"They've only recently opened up to international missions, actually. This is one of the first."

Her eyes widened in surprise. "Oh, that's cool."

"Yeah. Obviously, there are a few more legal and diplomatic hurdles to doing this kind of thing off US soil."

She nodded. "Yes. I'm glad you came. I can't imagine what would've happened if my parents had left me there."

She shivered. Against his better judgment, Mike wrapped an arm around her. She immediately let her head fall on his shoulder, where he couldn't see her mouth. No vibrations ran through her to indicate she was still talking, so they stayed that way for a while, taking comfort in each other.

After a while, Jessica yawned. Mike caught it, his jaw clicking with his own wide yawn.

"We should sleep. It'll be a long day tomorrow."

Jessica nodded and slowly raised her head. He wondered if she was as reluctant to part as he was, or whether it was his imagination.

He stood and dug through his pack, eventually producing a few sets of clothing, a bar of soap, and toothbrush and toothpaste.

"You need to get changed," he told her.

She frowned at him. "Why?"

"We should wash and dry those clothes you have on overnight, so you can wear them tomorrow. You need to be covered from the bugs tonight, but we'll sweat with this humidity. Better to wear one set of clothes every night, and have another for during the day."

She eyed him oddly, but eventually held out her hand. He draped the clothes over her arm, and handed her some bug spray.

"For once you're clean."

"You had this all along and you still smeared me with mud?"

Mike shrugged, unrepentant. "It was at the bottom of my back and we didn't have much time. I didn't want to take everything out and have to put it back in. But we can use it from now on."

She glared at him, but didn't say anything else, so he handed her the toiletries.

"That's all I've got," he told her. "So we'll have to share the toothbrush."

She ran a tongue over her teeth. "Honestly, I'm so filthy right now I'd share a toothbrush with a jaguar." She glanced up as if one might appear above her.

He grinned. "Well, I don't think I'm quite that bad."

"These clothes are so gross. Can I wear them tonight and wear these clean ones tomorrow?"

He shook his head. "These are mine. They'll be too big and uncomfortable for you to walk in. Better to sleep in these and keep your real clothes for the daytime."

She gave a reluctant nod, and then headed in the direction of the small stream. It lay at the edge of the firelight, and Mike forced himself not to watch as Jessica stripped off. Instead, he focused on gathering enough sticks to last them through the night, struggling to find many that were dry enough. It was easiest to survive in a jungle than any other climate. There was an abundance of food, water, and shelter if you knew where to look. But he sure did miss the area near where he'd grown up.

It had plenty of food to hunt, and dry wood for fires. He and his father had regularly gone on hunting trips, bringing back meat enough to feed the family for another week or two. Mike had two siblings, both younger. A brother and a sister. Neither of them had left town like he had. They'd stayed to repeat their parents' mistakes.

He should call them when he got back. He didn't hate them, he never had. But he didn't have much in common with any of his family, not since he'd moved away. He wanted them to move, too. Join him in Portsboro, where Soldiering On was located. But every time he suggested it, another argument sparked.

They hadn't understood why he'd wanted to leave, and he couldn't understand why they'd stayed.

But they were still family. And he should make more of an effort to stay in contact with them. Otherwise he might end up like Jessica, where she and her parents mutually used each other for their own benefit.

Jessica finally returned, scrubbed clean from hair to toes and in his clothes. She was fresher and happier now, even as she clutched sopping fabric to her chest. Mike was distracted by her wearing his clothes. They were too big for her, but a primal satisfaction welled in him at the sight regardless.

"I'll never take soap and toothpaste for granted ever again," she said as he came closer. "All I could do was splash myself with the water but it was the closest thing I've had to a shower in over a week."

He grinned. "I've been there. I'm glad I packed a full bag, even though I thought we'd be out within a day."

"Always be prepared?" she suggested.

"That's the Boy Scouts," he said with a laugh. "But yes."

He held out his hands for her clothes and then hung them over a low fern near the fire. They steamed instantly, and he hoped they'd be reasonably dry before morning. It was one of the challenges of jungle environment—avoiding the problems that came with being constantly damp.

"Want a boost?" he asked, nodding towards the hammock. He'd tied them at his chest height, higher off the ground than normal, knowing it was safer to be as far from the forest floor as possible.

She glanced over at it. She must have started speaking while her head was turned, because he only caught the tail end as she faced him again. "…struggle a little bit."

He strode forward and swept her up into his arms, bridal style. She whacked him on the chest.

"Hey!"

"You said you'd struggle," he said, pausing but not letting her down even when she squirmed. Her moving against him made his cock heavy, but he ignored it, focusing on her mouth.

"I *said*, 'I'm determined to do it myself, but I might struggle a bit.'"

"Well, how was I to know that? You were facing away."

She stopped squirming. "Oh." Her cheeks went red, visible even in the warm glow of the fire. "Sorry. I forgot for a moment."

"It's okay," he said. And it was. It took people a while to get used to facing him when they spoke. "Want me to put you down?"

She turned to the hammock, and then back to him. After a moment's hesitation, she shook her head and wrapped her arms around his neck. He pulled her even closer to him and stepped forward again, finally easing her into the hammock. It should hold, but he wouldn't take any chances that putting her down too heavily would send her straight onto her ass.

"How is it?" he asked dubiously.

"More comfortable than being tied to a chair," she told him with a smile.

He grinned at her. "Okay. I'll get ready for bed. See you in the morning. If you hear anything during the night, throw something at me. Your aim is pretty good."

Her grin widened. "I played softball in college, much to my parents' disgust. I picked the least graceful sport that had a women's team at my college."

"Well, don't hesitate to use those skills on me if you need to."

"I won't. Good night."

He nodded and took the toiletries from her. He headed towards the stream while she made herself comfortable. He cleaned off the day's sweat and dirt as best he could and then changed into clean clothes. He only had the three sets, so he had to hope nothing happened to these or they'd both be in trouble.

Once he'd cleaned his teeth and readied himself for the night, he returned to the camp. Jessica was already out like a light. No surprise, given the day's adventures. He hoped she had a good night's sleep, because she'd need her strength tomorrow, and for the week ahead.

He vaulted up into his own hammock, careful where he put his hands on the trees. He didn't want to accidentally stick his hand in a fire ant colony or hornet's nest.

When he was finally settled in the hammock he lay back and closed his eyes.

Then immediately snapped them open again.

He didn't like the vulnerability of being deaf in an unsafe, unfamiliar environment. With his eyes closed, then rebels could sneak up on them and take Jessica without him being the slightest bit aware.

He simply had to hope he'd taken enough precautions, and she'd be safe for the night. There was nothing more he could do.

He forced his eyes shut again, and willed his body to sleep. He'd need to be well rested, to be on the top of his game to keep Jessica safe. She deserved that much.

And finally, after a long moment, he fell into a restless slumber.

CHAPTER SIX

Parrots screeched.

Jessica woke with a start and tumbled out of her hammock, landing hard on her side. She lay in the dirt for a moment, groaning and trying to get her bearings.

When it all came back to her—the kidnapping, the trek through the jungle, *Mike*—she let out a long breath. And then scrambled into a sitting position as she remembered his warning about chigoes living in the earth.

She pulled herself up using the hammock and then glared at the trees above her. Damn parrots. It was too early for this. But then she lost her breath and the anger drained out of her at the sight of the stunning, bright colors flying above her. It was too high up for her to see much detail, but the reds and yellows flashed past her eyes, circling overhead. They were beautiful, if loud.

Though…she glanced around. It was quite light beneath the trees, so it was well past dawn. She must have slept for at least nine hours. It wasn't enough to make up for the lack of sleep for the last week, but between the sleep and the toothpaste, she definitely felt more human. And less likely to cry again.

Heat flooded her cheeks at the remembrance of her weakness. What must Mike think of her, losing it like that? Though, he hadn't commented on it, or berated her. In fact, he'd been quite sweet. Her cheeks heated as the memory of his hard arms around her surged.

She slanted a glance to his hammock, where he still slept peacefully. Clearly, the parrots hadn't disturbed his sleep. Lucky bastard. Well, if he planned to sleep in, she'd make herself useful. He deserved the sleep as much as she had.

Unable to resist the stream, Jessica headed over to splash water on her face. Even the nights were hot under the canopy, so she was sweaty all over again. Clearly, sweat would be a permanent fixture until she got out of here.

Once she returned to their makeshift camp, she took a deep drink of water from the pot they'd boiled last night. She was glad she'd kicked her coffee addiction a few years ago. She'd needed it to get through college, but after that, she'd spent a majority of her time in countries where resources like coffee were often scarce.

She stretched and her stomach grumbled. She could find some food, right? She shouldn't rely on Mike for everything.

She hunted through the trees for various fruits, like the papaya. She craved meat, or maybe nuts—some kind of protein, anyway. But she wasn't game to attempt setting traps or catching anything. That was definitely Mike's department. He could be the hunter, and she the gatherer, though she was a little loathe to comply with ancient gender roles.

A tree with an apple-like fruit grew near the campsite, so Jessica plucked a few from the branches. She pulled up the bottom of Mike's over-sized t-shirt to make a sling, and plopped the fruit into her makeshift basket. Next, she found some papayas, so she added those to the pile. A few feet away, a plant a bit like an orange grew, so she grabbed those, too. She was reaching for a strange-looking segmented fruit like a mini pumpkin when a hand grabbed her wrist.

Jessica squeaked and dropped the fruit as she spun around. She raised a hand, ready to fight off whoever held her.

Mike.

She slumped.

"You scared me."

"Sorry," he said, sharp-eyed despite the fact he must have just woken up. "I didn't want you to touch the sap."

She frowned. "What?"

"The sap on the tree you were reaching for," he said, indicating with his chin. "It's called a sandbox tree. The sap can irritate skin. And if you accidentally get it in your eyes, it can temporarily blind you."

Jessica froze. "Seriously?"

"Seriously," he confirmed, with a completely straight face. "We've already got a deaf guy. I don't want to risk having a blind woman in the party, too," he joked.

The blood drained from Jessica's face. "I had no idea. I'm sorry."

He shrugged. "It's fine. Just…don't touch this plant. The fruit is poisonous as well."

"Oh," Jessica said, shoulders hunching. "I didn't know. But I got some other stuff, too."

She glanced at the sad pile at her feet. Mike studied it as well, facing twisting like he was trying not to laugh. "Great job on the papaya," he said.

Jessica narrowed her eyes. "Are you saying those other fruits are poisonous, too?" she moaned.

He chuckled, like he could help it, and she scrunched her nose in apology. After a minute, she giggled along with him, his amusement infectious.

When he was finally done, he crouched down, and Jessica joined him.

"This one," he said, pointing to the apple-like fruit, "Is a beechapple. It's poisonous. This one," he said, indicating the orange-like fruit, "Is strychnine."

"Wait, like the poison?"

"Exactly like the poison. It's in the seeds. Mostly this plant is found in India, but like the bamboo, it's migrated across the world."

"Oh. So the only edible thing here is the papaya?"

"Yes."

She sighed. "Oh. I was so looking forward to some variety."

"We can find some other fruits," he assured her. "Why don't you grab more papaya from where you found it, and I'll meet you back at the camp? I want to get moving soon, but we need to eat."

She nodded and picked up the papaya from the pile. She headed back to the tree where she'd found them and picked some more with a sigh. She already never wanted to see another papaya, and she'd barely even eaten them before yesterday.

Had it really only been yesterday? So much had happened since then. Enough for a lifetime. But it had only been twenty-four hours or so since she'd met Mike.

After what they'd been through, it was already like they'd known each other for a lifetime, but really she knew so little about him. He'd opened up about his upbringing last night, and his job. It wasn't much, but it was a start. She was definitely curious to grill him some more about those things. What was his family like? What kinds of jobs did a security company like Soldiering On usually do? She couldn't imagine that dramatic rescues in foreign countries were the norm.

Jessica made it back to camp, her mind still on Mike. She threw more sticks on the fire, and then dumped her papayas on the raincoat they'd sat on the night before.

She took another drink of water—the day was already hot, and she knew she could easily dehydrate despite the moisture in the air.

Mike came back not long after, shirt full of fruits. "Guava and passion fruit," he told her. "Brazil nuts. I found some cashews as well, so I'll cook those while we eat."

Jessica let out a breath in relief.

They sat side-by-side. Mike cut the fruits with his knife, and handed half to Jessica before taking a bite himself. They alternated fruits and Brazil nuts as the cashews roasted merrily in a small pot. When Jessica was satisfied, she held up a hand to stop Mike from giving her any more.

He frowned. "Eat more."

"I've had enough."

"You need to eat more than enough. I'm not sure when we'll be able to stop, and we can't take the fruit with us. It'll go bad too quickly in the heat. It's better for you to overeat to get enough nutrients for the day."

Jessica reluctantly took some more guava from him. He saved the rest of the Brazil nuts and added them to the cashews, then finished off the rest of the fruit himself. He kept handing her slices, and Jessica ate whatever he gave her until she was full to bursting.

When she held up a hand again, he reluctantly stopped. "It won't fill you up for long," he warned.

"Truly, I can't eat another bite."

He nodded and stood. He kicked the remainder of the fruit and the skins deeper into the jungle. The hammocks caught his eye, and he paused.

"We should take these with us. I doubt we'll find more bamboo on our journey."

Though the hammock hadn't been her most comfortable night of sleep ever, it was still better than the dirt. Jessica stood to help him pull the hammocks down. She reached for the vine, only to snatch her hand back. The vine had gone from green to yellow, and was in fact no longer a vine.

"Snake," she hissed, heart hammering, but she was facing away from Mike.

She backed away, unable to take her eyes from the creature in front of her. She backed into something solid and she jumped, whipping her head around. *Mike.*

She buried her face into his chest to hide from the snake and clutched at his shirt. His arms came around her, automatically offering comfort, even though he must be confused. She waved a hand in the snake's direction, hoping that would explain why she was suddenly shivering.

But Mike didn't say anything in response, only held her close, as she forcibly pulled herself together.

It was only a snake. It wouldn't hurt her. And if it did, she had no doubt Mike would deal with it as calmly as he dealt with everything else.

As her reason returned, she became distractingly aware of his hard body against hers. She sucked in a breath and focused on him, not on the slithery thing behind her.

How is it that Mike smelled good? They had no proper shower, and yet somehow he didn't have the odor of stale sweat, just the pleasant scent of natural man.

That wasn't fair. She must smell like she'd been rolling in a dumpster for the last week.

Her hands fisted in his shirt, tugging him closer. But not in fear this time. No, she wanted to better feel him against her. Those hard muscles of his torso against her soft breasts. The rise and fall of his chest, his exhalations against her hair.

She wanted to dip her tongue out and taste his skin. It would be salty, she was sure. *Delicious.*

"Jessica?" he asked, the sound rumbling through his chest.

She swallowed, her mind leaving the pleasant daydreams she'd been having and crashing back to Earth. And to the reason she was currently in Mike's arms.

Slowly, she tilted her head back. Her gaze met Mike's, inches away. Close enough to kiss. His expression was intense and heated as he stared down at her.

She shook herself, dragging herself all the way out of her fantasies. "*Snake*," she repeated.

Mike glanced over to where she pointed, face tense. But he relaxed when his gaze landed on the snake that had so frightened her.

"Oh, he's okay. That one won't hurt you."

She shook her head in disbelief, frozen into speechlessness, and gripped his shirt tighter. He glanced down to where she tugged at him, then back at her with a raised eyebrow.

"Not a snake fan, huh?"

She shook her head, heart in her throat. She really, *really* didn't like snakes.

"You can face down armed men out to kidnap you with barely a blink, but the snakes send you into fits?"

"They're *slimy*, okay?"

He laughed. "Okay, stand back. It'll get rid of him for you."

Jessica shook her head, eyes locked on the snake. Mike lay a hand over hers and slowly disentangled her fists from his shirt. He pushed her an arm's length away in the opposite direction to the snake, then placed his hands on her shoulders and stared deep into her eyes.

"Stay."

Jessica bristled, some of her fear disappearing as her annoyance surged. He couldn't order her around like a dog. But before she could give him a cutting response, he whirled away and faced the snake. He picked it up near its neck without hesitating and lifted it gently from where it had twisted around the vine. Then, he strode into the forest and disappeared.

A few seconds later, he was back. Sans snake.

Jessica breathed a sigh of relief. "It's gone?"

"It's gone," he confirmed.

"Thank you."

He nodded. "You're welcome. Though if at all possible, I'd recommend getting over your fear of snakes. That won't be the last one we see out here."

She shuddered. "I wish that were possible."

He shrugged and gave her a roguish grin. "Or, you could jump in my arms again. I won't complain."

She glared at him, her face heating. "I didn't *jump.*"

"There was a bit of jumping," he teased.

"Well, it won't happen again. I was startled, is all." She straightened her spine, projecting as much dignity as she could manage given she'd considered *licking* the man less than a minute ago.

"More's the pity," he said, which only made her blush harder. Was he only teasing her? Or was this attraction a two-way street? She'd caught him staring at her breasts yesterday, sure. But it was one thing for a man to zero in on a woman's breasts because they were there, and another for him to be attracted to her. Wasn't it? Or would she just be a warm and willing body for him?

And she was willing. She hadn't been this attracted to a man in, well, ever. And it shocked her, because he definitely was *not* her type. Or maybe this had been her type all along, and she hadn't known it. Maybe her former boyfriends—all slim, intellectual types—hadn't floated her boat as much as she'd believed at the time.

Jessica considered Mike. She wouldn't be adverse to a little fun together while they were trapped out here. If they could find her a shower, that was. No way did she intend to sleep with a guy without access to necessary hygiene.

But that's all it could be. Fun in the jungle. There's no way she could seriously date a guy like Mike. Could she? They lived very different lives. His life in Portsboro sounded full of action and excitement. He traveled the world rescuing people.

And Jessica was rarely home, since she was also traveling most of the time. Or, she used to. Now, she wasn't so sure exactly what she planned to do once she got home. Could she go back to that life, after having been kidnapped and held hostage? She wasn't sure.

So what *would* she do with herself? Well, that was the question. And could it involve a guy like Mike?

It was far too soon to tell. She needed to make decisions for herself first. If she found room for a man in her new life, there was no guarantee it would be a former paratrooper.

She shook herself. She shouldn't be thinking such things. Not now.

They finished packing up the camp. Jessica helped Mike strap the hammocks to his back, over his pack—no snakes this time.

They set off through the jungle once again.

Jessica's muscles complained twenty minutes into the walk and got progressively more vocal for the next hour. She hadn't known how sore she still was from the trek the day before until she forced those muscles to work again. Eventually, they loosened up enough that she wasn't gritting her teeth with every step.

Mike stopped them for a rest any time they encountered edible fruit—avoiding the ones she now knew to be poisonous. They quickly downed the sweet flesh, had a handful of the nuts he'd toasted earlier, and sipped some water from the supply he'd boiled the night before.

During one of these stops, Jessica slumped against a tree. "Must we go so fast?"

She was sweating in the heat, her clothes sticking to her skin. The wash she'd given them last night had helped a little, but she still fully intended to burn these clothes the instant she could find replacements.

"The slower we walk, the longer it'll take us to get to the border," he told her. "And the more vulnerable we'll be if the rebels are chasing us. We can rest when we're safe."

Jessica knew all that, she did. But she was ready to collapse right here and she had at least six more days to go. Mike, too, was affected by the heat and enforced exercise. Dark shadows smudged beneath his eyes and his skin glistened with sweat. He took another long sip of water and handed the canteen back to her.

"It'll be dark in a few hours," he continued. "I'll start looking for a place to stop, so we don't have to make camp in the dark."

Jessica nodded gratefully. When Mike called time on the break, she reluctantly straightened from the tree and followed him deeper into the jungle.

The worst of it was that there was nothing to distract her, and she was *bored*. She couldn't talk to Mike—he couldn't read her lips from where she was behind him. When she'd go for a walk or to the gym back home, she'd always listen to a podcast or an audiobook to keep her entertained.

The rainforest was beautiful, and unique. There were millions of species of plants and animals surrounding her. But after a while, the greenery faded into an overwhelming blur.

Her mind darted between her week in captivity, to her uncertain future, and back again. Sometimes her brain gave her a reprieve by focusing on Mike—mostly on his ass, if she was honest—which was a nice distraction from her circular thoughts.

Finally, Mike called a halt as the light dimmed. Jessica glanced around the campsite he'd chosen. It was a small area—too small to even be called a clearing—surrounded by trees and chest-height ferns. Beyond the trees, to her right, was a pond. She couldn't see in the fading light, but she suspected it was connected to a river farther along, because the water was temptingly clear.

"I'm going for a swim," she announced, eyes riveted on the pond. Anticipation thrummed through her. Finally, she could properly clean off all the dirt and sweat that had accumulated on her skin.

She took a step towards the water, eyes focused on the pond as if she approached the gates of heaven. Mike's arm shot out, stopping her in her tracks. She glanced at him in question.

"No, you won't," he told her.

She narrowed her eyes. "Why not?" She wanted that swim so bad.

"This kind of place is perfect for piranhas. Leeches. Even electric eels. There are probably candiru in the water, too."

"What the hell is a candiru?"

"It's an Amazonian catfish. About this big," he said, holding his fingers about an inch apart.

"Well, that doesn't sound so bad."

"Apparently they've been known to swim up people's urethras and get stuck. They're barbed."

Jessica sucked in a breath as a pang of sympathy pain struck her. Just like that, she had no desire to go swimming anymore. She could weep in frustration. So close to true cleanliness and yet so far.

"That sounds unpleasant," she said, stepping away from the water.

"Yeah. I've never seen it happen, but it sure isn't worth the risk."

Jessica shook her head enthusiastically. "Is everything in this jungle trying to kill us?" she lamented.

"Probably best to assume that, yes."

Jessica made a face. Well, they'd survived this far. She could survive another few days of misery if it meant getting to safety.

"I'll boil us some water," he said in an apologetic tone. "I know it's not the same, but it'll keep us clean enough for now."

"I suppose it means my shower—when I do get one—will be better the longer I wait." She said it on a sigh, wistful and not remotely convincing. Damn it, she really wanted to be properly clean.

She helped Mike take the hammocks off his back. He hung his bag on a tree notch, eyeing the ground suspiciously.

"Leeches," he explained, when he caught her watching him.

She shuddered.

Mike set up the camp, hanging the hammocks, starting the fire, and numerous other tasks Jessica couldn't decipher. Jessica dug through his pack and pulled out the pot he'd used to boil water the night before. She filled it with water, careful where she put her feet on the edge of the pond. Leeches, he'd said. Piranhas. Those gross catfish things.

She never wanted to come back to the rainforest again. During her travels, she'd spent plenty of times in tropical and sub-tropical countries. But she'd always stuck to the cities, and their outskirts. Places with some civilization, at least. The orphanage she'd been volunteering at had been outside of the city, but it had been accessible by road, and surrounded by cleared land. Not deadly things that could kill her given the slightest chance.

Until the rebels had kidnapped her, she'd never been this deep into a rainforest. Now that she'd had a taste of it, she had no intention of returning.

Once the fire burned, Jessica put the pot of water over it to boil. Mike disappeared for a few minutes and came back with a dead parrot.

"Please tell me that's not dinner," she said, eyeing the brightly-colored feathers.

"It's dinner. We need the protein."

"No arguments, but…a parrot?" She'd wanted meat, but she hadn't even known parrots were edible.

"What's wrong with the parrot? You're not a vegetarian, are you?"

She shook her head. "It's just so pretty." Not so much now that it was dead, but when she'd seen parrots exactly like that flying above her that morning, it hadn't occurred to her that she'd have to eat one.

"Pigs are cute, and we eat those."

She side-eyed him. "You think pigs are cute?"

"Don't you?"

"Piglets, maybe."

"Well, I like them."

She grinned at the defensive note in his voice. So the man had a soft spot for pigs? That was strangely adorable.

"You won't notice the parrot once I take the feathers off. Don't worry."

She sighed, but agreed. She needed to eat, and she couldn't be squeamish. As long as he wasn't feeding her snakes, she'd suck it up and deal with it.

The water finally boiled. "Can I use this to wash?" she asked.

Mike nodded. "You can grab the soap from my pack."

She dug her hand into the bag, searching for the soap she'd used the night before. She dug a little deeper, and her hand encountered something she couldn't identify. She tugged it out, only to find it was a coin she didn't recognize.

She turned back to Mike. He'd already plucked the feathers from the parrot and was preparing to roast it on a spit above the fire.

She waved to catch his eye and he glanced up. "What's this?" she asked.

He frowned in confusion before his gaze shifted to the coin in her hand. "Just my lucky coin." His gaze shuttered, as if there was more to the story that he didn't want to tell.

"I wouldn't have pegged you as the superstitious type," Jessica commented.

He shrugged. "I think all soldiers are, a little. If by some miracle you survive a firefight, or a bomb blast, you want to believe it was through something you can control, rather than it being pure luck. Yourself, your team, what socks you wore that day. The photo of the girl you left back home. Anything."

Jessica swallowed. "Did you have a girl you left back home?" The question popped out against her will, and she wasn't even sure she wanted the answer. For all she knew, he *still* had a girl he'd left back home.

"No," he answered. "Didn't seem right to make someone wait for me. So I stuck to short-term things any time I was back stateside."

She nodded. That, Jessica understood. She spent most of her time volunteering in foreign countries. Sometimes, in moments of weakness, she thought it might be nice to have someone to return home to, or travel with. But what man would put up with a girlfriend or wife that was gone more than half the year? Only one man she'd liked enough to suggest he come with her, but he'd refused.

"But you've been out for a while, now. You must be stateside for much longer stretches."

He nodded. "Sure. I guess I haven't met the woman who makes me want to settle down, yet. Between my recovery and new job, I haven't had a lot of time to think about relationships. "

Her heart lurched. She didn't know why she should care whether or not Mike was the settling down type, but his words still affected her. If he was a short-term guy, that should work out for her. She only did short term, these days. And a fling suited her fine.

But the ache in her heart didn't disappear when she reminded herself of that.

She searched for a change in conversation topic, landing on the coin still in her hand. "So you believe this coin got you through the war?"

His lips twisted. "It didn't hurt." There was a story there. One of pain. But he clearly had no intention of telling her about it.

She slipped the coin back into the bag and pulled out the soap. "I'll be on the other side of the ferns," she told him.

He nodded, then stood to carry the water for her.

"You don't have to do that."

She didn't know whether he didn't see her statement or if he ignored her, but either way he didn't reply. He placed the water down and then turned to her. The light from the fire barely reached them, and she wondered if he could still see her lips.

"If you see any more snakes, I won't hear you scream," he said. "So keep your eyes open." There was a teasing light in his eyes, now. Clearly, he'd moved on from whatever had caused the shadows in his eyes at the sight of the coin.

He returned to camp, leaving her in darkness. She washed hurriedly, her imagination providing plenty of images of snakes and other creepy crawlies coming at her from the darkness. The light from the fire wasn't enough behind the ferns. She should've brought Mike's flashlight.

She threw her clothes back on and pushed back through the ferns and into the warm glow of the fire. The cold shiver down her spine from the unnerving darkness quickly warmed once she crouched near the flames.

"Your turn," she told Mike.

He nodded and disappeared in the direction she'd come from, returning not long after with damp hair. He threw the leftover water back into the pond and scooped up some more. He checked the bird.

"Not long now. We'll boil more water once it's done."

Her stomach grumbled and she nodded.

Mike picked up some papaya from his lap and squeezed in onto the roasting parrot, as if he'd already done it a few times while she wasn't paying attention.

"Wait, papaya flavored parrot?" she asked.

He grinned. "It tenderizes tough meat."

"Huh. You learn something new every day." Jessica wasn't a great cook. Her parents had always had a cook to prepare their meals for them, and Jessica had never been allowed in the kitchen to learn. As an adult, she spent so little time at home, she never bothered.

While they waited for the parrot to finish cooking, they talked of other, less personal things.

The way Mike stared at her lips as she talked sent a tingle down her spine that, this time, wasn't from fear.

There was something about the intensity of his gaze, the heat in his eyes, that warmed her from the inside out.

But a jungle wasn't the place for a fling.

Was it?

CHAPTER SEVEN

Mike woke first this time.

Jessica still slumbered peacefully on the hammock opposite him, and he didn't have the heart to wake her. She needed the rest. He'd pushed her hard for two days and she hadn't complained, despite the fact that she must be hurting. He admired that.

Admired *her*.

But he didn't need to be thinking about that. About her strength, and bravery. About her beauty. It's not like anything could happen between them while they were in the jungle. And after? Well, maybe a quick fling. Something to burn away the chemistry between them. But nothing more. Never anything more.

Mike wasn't the settling down type. He'd never been tempted, not really. And maybe that was because he never got to know a woman well enough to think about a future with her, or maybe that's the way he was built.

Jessica was the wrong kind of woman to practice relationships with. They were from such different worlds. Her, from one of the richest families in America, and him from one of the poorest. He'd never fit in with her life.

Not that he wanted to try.

Mike shook off the circular, pointless thoughts. He needed to concentrate on getting Jessica into Colombia safely, and nothing else mattered.

It worried him that they hadn't seen any signs of pursuit. They'd been pushing hard, but the rebels had more manpower than him and Jessica. Surely they couldn't be too far behind. Had they given up hope of grabbing Jessica and the money she represented? Or had the rebels found another way to track them?

He couldn't rely on the idea that they'd given up, that they'd let him and Jessica cross the border without putting up a fight. So he'd have to operate under the assumption that the rebels were still coming for them—he just didn't know which direction it would be from.

Maybe…he glanced at the tree towering above him, the one with his hammock tied to it. The low branches meant it wouldn't be too difficult to climb, and it might help him get a better lay of the land.

He didn't waste any time, vaulting into the lower branches and hauling himself up. He climbed, ignoring the ache in his shoulders from carrying his heavy pack, until he was as high as the tree would take him. He wasn't near the canopy, but the trunk smoothed out above him, making it impossible to climb without gear.

Now that he was higher, the lush undergrowth no longer restricted his view. The trunks of the surrounding trees meant he couldn't see too far into the distance, but he could at least be certain none of the rebels were nearby. The only movement came from birds and other animals, above and below.

He turned the opposite way, to the direction they headed in. Still not a lot of visibility, but a river snaked in the distance. Hopefully it would turn away, so they wouldn't have to cross it.

Mike stayed up there a few moments longer, enjoying the view. Then, unable to delay much longer, he shimmied down the tree.

Jessica still hadn't woken, and Mike found his gaze repeatedly drawn to her as he readied breakfast. She was stunningly beautiful, of course, but he preferred her wide awake and with flashing eyes. Even if she was kicking him in the nuts.

He grinned at the memory. Yeah, she had fire. And he liked that in a woman.

A little too much. He'd almost told her the story of the coin last night. And he'd never told anyone that story. It was too personal, and still cut deep into his soul. Every time he remembered that day it made his chest squeeze tight with anger and grief and guilt and a horrible kind of relief. Too complicated to explain to anyone, including himself.

When breakfast was ready, Mike strode over to Jessica. He hesitated a moment before waking her, gaze roaming over her face, drinking her in. Then, he shook himself, and squeezed her shoulder.

Her eyes snapped open. Worry quickly turned into a soft smile when she saw it was him. The expression was a punch to his gut, and he could imagine her giving him that same smile every morning, maybe after a long night of lovemaking.

"Hey," she said, then yawned.

"Hey," he said, swallowing thickly. Forcing his brain to focus.

"Breakfast?" she asked hopefully.

He nodded and stepped away from her. She rose, stretched, headed to the bathroom behind the ferns, and then returned as he was setting out more fruit for her.

"I hate to say it, but I miss the parrot," she told him, eyeing the papaya and guava.

He grinned. "I'll catch some more for dinner tonight. But, for now, we have to get moving."

She nodded and straightened her spine, eating the fruit and nuts without complaint. Once they were ready—the hammocks once again strapped to his back—they set off through the dense undergrowth.

Mike kept away from the river he'd seen, but followed its path. Since the canopy broke above the water, the sunlight made the plants grow more lushly close to the water's edge. He didn't want to waste precious energy hacking through thicker undergrowth if he didn't have to. The damp ground was perfect for leeches, too, and he didn't relish the idea of dealing with those. He made sure both he and Jessica had their shin guards strapped on tightly, so no creatures would crawl up their pant legs and make a home.

The stream they were following eventually joined with a much larger river—the opposite of what he'd been hoping for. He paused on the riverbank and surveyed the rushing water. Thirty feet across, with a steep bank of plants on the other side. Not ideal. Not even close.

Jessica tapped his shoulder. "Will we have to cross this?"

"Yes."

"How? Swim it?"

He shook his head. "Could be crocodiles in there. Piranhas. Leeches. And the water is deceptively fast. I'd bet if we jumped in we'd be carried straight downstream, the opposite of where we need to go."

"So how will we do it?"

"That's what I'm figuring out." If they had three people, he might risk it. That way they could swim across one at a time, with a rope or vine around the two on shore, anchoring them. But with only the two of them—and the possibility of deadly animals in the water, Mike was loathe to risk it.

She tilted her head. "Huh."

"What?" he asked.

"That's the first time you haven't had a plan."

He shrugged. He wouldn't admit to her that he'd been making everything up as he went along, ever since the airport. He'd counted on Charlie flying them out of there. He hadn't expected to be traipsing through the Amazon for a week, with barely any supplies.

"Can you build a boat?" she asked.

He shook his head. "I mean, I could probably build a raft. But it could easily get swept away with the current. And if there *are* crocodiles in there, I doubt anything I could make would win in a fight against their teeth."

"Oh," she said, eyes wide.

"Are you a strong swimmer?" he asked.

She wrinkled her nose. "I can't outswim a crocodile, if that's what you're asking."

He grinned. "Just want to know what I'm working with."

"I'm okay. I can do some laps, no problem. But like I said, I was a softball girl in college."

He eyed her. "I wouldn't have expected that." He didn't know why he said that. She'd already told him she'd chosen softball to annoy her parents. But the strange feelings for her that he was unable to exorcise—no matter how hard he tried—were making him contrary.

He wanted to find a reason to dislike her. It would make everything far easier. Then, he wouldn't miss her when they inevitably parted ways after the jungle. But so far, the only thing he didn't like about her was her wealth, so he focused on that, hoping it would break this spell.

"From a rich girl, you mean?" She raised her eyebrows, challenging him to answer. Her eyes were bright, as if she enjoyed the teasing as much as he did. Well, Mike had never backed down from a challenge.

"Yeah, from a rich girl. Didn't you want to play tennis, or…I don't know. Croquet?" He didn't think he could ever like someone who played croquet.

She snorted a laugh. "I think you're over a hundred years too late on the croquet fad."

"You know what I mean."

"I do. You have an image of what rich people are like," she told him boldly. Mike's jaw clenched at how easily she'd read him. "And, yeah, a lot of my friends played more typical sports. But I wanted to annoy my parents."

He narrowed his eyes. "So it was genuinely just teenage rebellion?"

"Basically," she replied, unrepentant. "I mean, I liked the sport, too. But if there had been a rugby team, or something even less girly that allowed female players, I would have picked that."

He considered her for a long moment, an itch forming in his gut. The heat, the chemistry, between them…could that be rebellion, too? Was she thinking about how getting with the white trash soldier would annoy her parents?

It would make sense, and explain why a woman like her was flirting with him. Maybe she wanted to have a fling in the jungle with the man her parents had hired, simply to annoy them. Wasn't that a thing rich people did? Sleep with the help as a power play?

Or was he again searching for reasons not to like this woman? He couldn't even tell anymore. And why should it even matter if she only wanted a fling to piss off her parents? He'd never had a problem with that kind of thing before. In fact, it usually worked well for him—a short-term affair, and a middle finger to the rich—two of his favorite things.

But for some reason, it did matter to him when it came to Jessica. And he refused to look too deeply to figure out why.

Frustrated by his train of thought, Mike gave her a tight smile.

"We'll have to keep walking until we find a bridge."

Hopefully there was one. This deep into the rainforest, there was a good chance no one would bother. But if there were native tribes in the area, they might get lucky and find a way to cross.

"How long do you think that will take?" Jessica asked.

"It might add another day to our journey." At a minimum, but he didn't want to freak her out yet.

She sighed, but nodded, looking only mildly disappointed. Again, no complaints, simply a willingness to do the hard work to get home. He almost wished she would complain, make herself more annoying. Then, he'd like her less, and this strange ache in his chest would stop.

Or maybe he wanted her to cry again, so he'd have an excuse to take her into his arms and hold her tight.

Shit, he didn't know what he wanted.

They set off again. Mike kept closer to the river now, even though it made pushing through the undergrowth more tiring. He didn't want to miss a bridge across the water. The river bent a few times, but mostly stayed in a straight line.

It wasn't wet season, thank God, or the rain would be monsoonal and the river would be swollen even further. He could see the water line on some of the trees, and suspected most of this area would be underwater once the rains came in.

After a full day's hike, they still hadn't found a bridge, so Mike finally admitted defeat as the last of the daylight faded. It was an entire day wasted, but there was nothing he could do to make it go faster, not without risking himself or Jessica.

Impatience dogged at him. He wanted Jessica home and safe. And he wanted her far away from him where she couldn't cause these unfamiliar sensations in his chest.

They set up camp, a few feet back from the riverbank. They had a routine now. Getting the fire set up, the food trapped, the water boiling. Washing up before dinner, and hanging the hammocks.

Changing into their sleeping clothes and rinsing out the day's sweat from their walking outfit.

"Parrot again," she commented, making a face. He squeezed papaya onto the sizzling skin and grinned.

"I could maybe find us a monkey. Or even a snake."

She gave a full-body shiver. "Parrot is great," she said unconvincingly.

He glanced back at the cooking bird again and turned it slowly. He'd had worse. Fresh food, regardless of what it was, had to be better than the MREs—Meals Ready to Eat—they survived on in the military.

Jessica waved her hand, grabbing his attention.

"Yeah?"

"Aren't there fish in the river?" she said, indicating to the river behind a cluster of ferns.

"Probably."

"And wouldn't those be easier to catch than a parrot?"

"Sure. And I might at some point. But they are also more likely to be infected with parasites."

Jessica rolled her eyes. "What the hell is it with this place?"

Mike chuckled. "I know I make it sound awful, but I'm only being careful. The jungle really is the best place to survive. We've got water, food, shelter. Sure, there are some difficulties, but compared to being lost in a desert, or a snow storm, we've got it good out here."

"I suppose so. Wouldn't the locals survive on fish, though? In most places I've been to, the poorest people live off the land as much as possible, and fish should be plentiful."

"Yes, but their bodies are probably used to the various bacteria around here. We aren't local, so our stomachs won't like it. And the locals might be responsible for the parasites if they dump their waste into the river. There could be tapeworm and stuff."

"How do you know all this?" she asked, staring at him in astonishment. "It's like you know everything about this place, every danger. Is this a common vacation destination for you or something?"

Mike laughed and shifted on his raincoat. Jessica sat across the fire on the pack, where he could see her face more easily. He had to concentrate, since the light was low, which he knew meant he'd be staring at her intensely. But Jessica either didn't notice, or didn't mind.

"Obviously, I've been to a lot of interesting places in the military. And we get handbooks we have to study. But mostly I just like to read."

"Huh. Nonfiction mostly, I presume?"

He cleared his throat. "Yeah." He didn't know why he was reluctant to admit he liked to read. It wasn't an unusual hobby, after all. But after years of being sneered at for his love of books, it still felt like a dirty little secret. No one in his community had prized book learning, since all of the jobs in the area were working class. What was the point of learning stuff that wasn't necessary? They acted like he was looking down on everyone else.

He came from a poor town, and his public school education left a lot to be desired. No doubt Jessica had attended all the best private schools. He couldn't compete with that, not on an intellectual level.

"I read a lot of politics and current affairs," she told him. "Biographies. I do read some fiction, sometimes. Romance, mostly. To escape, you know? But it's often set in such a different world to the one I know. I can't get into it."

He nodded. He knew what that was like. Particularly right after he'd come back from his last tour. He'd read books to distract himself. Most were too frothy and unrealistic, featuring characters with petty problems that were nothing compared to what he'd survived. Other genres, like thrillers or crime, often glorified the violence he'd escaped.

In nonfiction, at least, he learned something, without worrying too much about realism or entertainment.

"You must have seen some things in your volunteer work," Mike said suddenly. He hadn't considered that before now, still thinking of Jessica as the spoiled socialite. But her charity work took her to some of the places in the world that suffered the most.

She nodded, her face harsh. "I've watched children dying from hunger and preventable diseases. I think that's the worst thing. And doing everything you can, only to find sometimes it's not enough."

Mike swallowed. Shit, it really was like his time in the military. The helplessness, the pain. They had more shared experiences than he'd expected.

"How long do you think you can do it?" he asked softly.

Tears sprang to her eyes. "I don't know. I honestly don't know."

He nodded. "Part of me is glad I was forced out when I was. Before I was too broken by what I saw."

Jessica gave him a look so full of understanding it broke his heart. He didn't want her to know what that was like. She turned away and wiped her eyes, so Mike turned his attention to the cooking parrot to give her an illusion of privacy. It was ready, so busied himself taking it off the fire. From the corner of his eye, he noticed her turn back to him and straighten her spine, as if determined to put the conversation aside.

"Ready to eat?" he asked.

She nodded, so he dished out the food between them and returned to his seat opposite her. As far as he could get, in the hope she wouldn't tempt him. It didn't work.

They were silent as they ate. It was too difficult for him to carry on a conversation over meals. Food and fingers hovered in front of the mouth, blocking his view. Chewing distorted the mouth shapes, so he couldn't understand.

When they were full and had washed their hands and faces, they returned to their positions around the fire. It was too early to sleep. Clearly, their bodies were getting used to the exercise, since they weren't as exhausted as they had been the previous two nights.

Jessica shifted, drawing his attention. "So, I didn't ask, but the lip reading thing. How does it work?"

Mike relaxed at the new topic. This was far easier ground.

"I watch the movement of your lips, tongue, face, and so on. I can grasp about one in three of the words you say, and I piece together the rest from there. People who gesture a lot or are really expressive are easier to read, because there are more clues and context."

"How long did it take you to learn?"

"Honestly? I'm still learning. It takes a while. But I get by."

"Are some people easier to read than others?"

"Yeah. People who mumble are a nightmare. You speak clearly, so I haven't had much trouble so far."

"All those elocution lessons my parents sent me to finally paid off," she said with a smile.

His eyebrows shot up. "You went to elocution lessons?"

She laughed. "No, but you believed me. You have some weird ideas about rich people."

Mike chuckled. He loved that she made fun of herself and her upbringing. "I guess I do. But, seriously, there are a lot of reasons lip reading can be tough. It's harder now in the low light of the fire, particularly this far away. It's hard if the person is tired or drunk and slurring their words. Beards and mustaches make it trickier. Someone with an accent or thin lips can be more difficult. We're lucky I find you easy to understand or it might get messy."

"Would it be easier for you to see my lips if I sat closer?"

Mike swallowed, unable to breathe for a second. Her face hadn't changed, not really, but there was a subtle shift that told him her mind had gone somewhere else, somewhere flirtatious. Did he want to encourage that, encourage her?

No.

"Yeah."

She immediately stood and rounded the fire. She parked herself next to him on the raincoat and crossed her legs. He couldn't take his eyes off her. Not only in case she said anything, but because of the soft glow of the fire over her pale skin. She was so beautiful in this light. In all lights, if he was honest.

"Have you ever had a really embarrassing moment because you misunderstood something?"

"Oh yeah," he chuckled, dragging his mind away from his attraction to her. "Particularly when someone says something out of nowhere and you have no context for what they are saying. Once some guy with a long beard ran over to me. The street was dark, I could barely see his lips. All I could see was the panic in his eyes. And he says to me "Someone's stolen my sheep!"'" He paused, admiring the way Jessica's eyes lit in amusement. "Now, keep in mind this was in downtown Portsboro. Not too many sheep around. But he kept saying it. "You gotta help me, man. Someone stole my sheep." I thought he was high, offered to call a doctor."

She laughed. "And did you figure it out?"

"Yeah. Turns out that "sheep" and "Jeep" can look weirdly similar when an agitated, bearded man is yelling at you on a dark street."

Jessica threw her head back and laughed harder. Mike watched her, chest filling with an answering joy. But he wished, suddenly, that he could hear what that laughter sounded like.

He waited until her laughter died and she looked at him again, but the spark still hovered in her eyes. "I don't get everything you say, either. It's not really like hearing words, because there are so many variables to a human face. Seeing someone straight on, with good lighting, and a clear view helps, but it's not perfect."

"That's so fascinating," she said. "I never really thought of it like that. The movies make it look like magic." She leaned into his arm, her warm weight pressed against him. His skin tightened.

"I wish. I could be a super spy if it worked like that, reading the lips of enemy spies from miles away, while they have secret meetings."

"It wouldn't work like that? Even with binoculars?"

He shook his head. "Too far away. You could only get half of the conversation, focusing on one person at a time. And they probably wouldn't face straight on. I'd get a few words, but not enough to make it worthwhile. And I could easily mistake some important piece of information. It's easy to get things mixed up."

She nodded. "I guess, since we haven't really had any stumbles, it didn't occur to me how hard it must be for you."

He shrugged. "It's okay. Better than not communicating with people at all." She turned slightly, her breasts pressing into his arms. A shiver ran down his spine and his cock ached. She was trouble, this one. A simple, unconscious gesture from her and his body responded as if she was stripping naked in front of him. He wrenched his mind away from that image before it got too heated.

"Do you know sign language, too?"

"Yeah, I'm learning. I prioritized learning to lip read, so I could still hold onto my old life. I wanted to talk to the same people, in the same way I was familiar with. Stay in the hearing world."

"And now?"

"Well, with signing, sometimes it's easier. I get the whole picture, rather than snippets. I've made new friends who are deaf, and it's kind of a relief to talk in sign instead of piecing together half-formed words. But I'm not totally fluent yet."

"Can you teach me some?"

"Sign language?"

"What else can we do?" she teased, looking around the nearly-empty camp.

He almost didn't want to. It would be an odd kind of intimacy to teach her to sign, a whole new way of communicating. He'd be bringing her into his world, and connecting them in a whole new way. Out here, it would be like the two of them had their own secret language, even though there were about five hundred thousand other people who spoke ASL.

And if he was being honest, there was another way he'd prefer to communicate with her right now. A way that didn't involve words at all, spoken or signed. He wanted to kiss her, touch her. Communicate in that ancient, primal way.

He liked sex. He was glad that particular activity hadn't changed much after he lost his hearing. Sure, he missed hearing his partners' cries of pleasure, but a body could communicate so much without the need for words. A muscle contracting, a sheen of sweat, squirming against the bedsheets. All told him he was on the right track.

But he couldn't do that with Jessica. Not here and now. Not with rebels chasing them, and neither of them having had a shower in what was, frankly, far too long.

Once he got her home, and safe, they could act on their attraction if they were both still willing. Maybe. Hell, he wouldn't even mind if she was using him to piss off her parents. Wouldn't be the first time, and they'd both still get something out of it.

Though the words didn't ring true, even in his head. He didn't want that, not with her. They both deserved better.

Deserved more.

He shook his head to clear it and then focused back on Jessica. What had she asked? Oh, yes. Sign language.

"Okay. So, first thing you have to know is that the syntax is different for ASL than for spoken English. It's actually more similar to Japanese." He explained the structure of sentences while Jessica watched him closely.

"I think I can remember that." Her voice dropped as she repeated it to herself. "Time tense, subject, color, other adjectives, action."

"Right," he said, surprised by how seriously she was taking it. Most people only wanted to know the swear words. "But first, how about I teach you the letters and numbers, so you can fingerspell if you need to?"

She nodded enthusiastically. Then, she shuffled around on the raincoat so she faced him. Mike did the same, pressing his knees against hers to keep off the moist ground.

He went through each of the letters one by one, and repeated them again and again while she followed along until she almost had them perfect. She giggled each time she got one wrong, but still kept her focus, determined to get it right.

Next, they moved on to numbers. When they got to nine, she stopped him. "Wait, isn't that the sign for "f'?" She held up her hand, the index finger and thumb pressed together, the remaining three fingers sticking up.

He shook his head. "No, the one for "f" has these two fingers more rounded," he explained, brushing his fingers over hers. A tingle spread across his hand, but he ignored it. "The one for nine has them pressed more flat."

She blew out a breath. "Okay. That's confusing."

He stopped at ten, and then made her repeat the numbers back again. Then, the alphabet one more time.

"I think that's enough for one night," he said. His body was too heated from their proximity and constant contact. He needed a break before he did something he regretted, like kiss her senseless.

She nodded, then yawned. "It's learning a whole new language. I really had no idea."

"Yeah, it can be difficult." She was picking it up much faster than he had, though.

"Tomorrow you'll have to teach me some actual words," she said, bouncing with excitement.

He grinned with some bafflement. He thought she'd be bored after one session, but she seemed genuinely keen to learn more.

"Okay," he agreed.

They got ready for bed, Mike with a reluctance that surprised even him. He wanted to keep talking to Jessica, about anything and everything. He liked their nights by the fire. They could talk then, as opposed to when he led them through the rainforest. During the long, boring days, he missed chatting to her. Part of the reason he called halts so often is so he could have an excuse to look at her, speak with her.

He'd never been like this with a woman before and it was as frustrating as fuck. Sex, he could do. No dramas at all. But this strange ache building in his chest? He had no idea what to do with that.

All he could do for now was ignore it. Hell, he might ignore it even after they escaped this damn jungle. He didn't need complications in his life.

But did he want them?

Mike took a long time to fall asleep, his mind too full with Jessica.

CHAPTER EIGHT

Around lunchtime, they finally spotted a bridge in the distance. It looked sturdy, and Jessica breathed a sigh of relief at the idea that they'd soon be across the river and continuing their journey. Made of solid wood, it rose high above the river, likely because the water would swell dramatically in the rainy season.

Jessica took a step forward, a new spring in her step. Once they crossed that bridge they'd be moving forward again, instead of sideways. Closer to getting home—and to a shower.

But Mike wrapped an arm around her waist to stop her, yanking her against his hard body. Jessica half-turned towards him in outrage, even as she reveled in the sensation of being pressed against such a strong chest. The feel of him made her even hotter than the humidity did.

She opened her mouth to ask what the hell he was doing, but froze as he pressed a finger to his lips, telling her to be silent. She frowned in confusion and bristled at being told what to do. She huffed, but logic quickly returned and she obeyed. Had he seen something?

He released her, dragging his hand over her stomach as he moved away. Jessica shivered, but Mike didn't notice. He crept closer to the river, his footsteps quiet on the soft, springy earth. How did he avoid making sounds when he couldn't even hear himself? It was remarkable.

Mike pushed aside the ferns and peered across the river. Jessica's heart hammered in fear and confusion, but she didn't dare get closer to see whatever he was staring at. She had no confidence she could move as quietly as he had. What was across the river? Maybe he'd spotted a panther in the trees, or some other predator ready to attack.

The bridge was minutes away, and she itched to move and continue on their journey. So close. But she held herself still.

Finally, after what seemed like an age, Mike backed away from the river's edge and returned to her. He pressed his lips close to her ear, breath brushing over her skin. Her skin tightened at the sensation.

"The rebels are waiting for us on the other side."

It took a second for the words to penetrate her lust-addled mind, but as soon as they did, she stiffened. "What?" she hissed. Thankfully, the running water of the wide river drowned out the noise they might make, but she still made sure to keep her voice low.

"It's an ambush. They knew we'd need to cross the river eventually, and there are probably only so many bridges this deep in the jungle. I'm guessing they circled around once they lost us at the airport and have been waiting for us ever since."

Jessica's heart sank. It made sense. The rebels knew the jungle better than anyone. And since they had vehicles, they would've traveled quicker than Mike and Jessica, even if they had to hike some of the way. There were still some roads this deep in the rainforest, mostly for illegal loggers to use for their trucks. Jessica should've guessed the rebels would use them to get the drop on her and Mike.

"What can we do?" she asked, defeat creeping into her voice.

He shrugged. "I don't know how many are over there. I won't attack them head-on, particularly not when I can't do any recon. If I could get across the river and circle around, I might be in with a chance if I took them by surprise, but since this is the only bridge we know about I don't think that would work."

"You must have some kind of plan," she pleaded. "If we keep walking, we'll eventually come to another bridge, right?"

He nodded. "But I'm not sure how long it'll take to find it, particularly given how slow we're moving through the undergrowth. It could add weeks to our journey."

"Weeks?" she hissed. Oh, this was turning out to be a total disaster. She wanted to sink to the forest floor in defeat. She'd die out here, like a hamster on a treadmill that couldn't dismount. She'd keep walking forever as the jungle threw more obstacles in her path until she accepted her fate.

He gazed steadily back at her, an ocean of calm. Warmth radiated from him, crossing the small gap between them. Despite the heat in the air, she took comfort from it, from him. Surely this wasn't it? Surely she wouldn't have to return to the rebels after all this work?

"I guess there's nothing else we can do, right?"

He squeezed her hand. "Maybe we'll get lucky. You never know."

Her heart tumbled. By now, Jessica should want to be a million miles away from him, if her previous relationship experiences were anything to go by. Instead, she wanted nothing more to stay by his side, even after they left this damned jungle.

They set off, Jessica conscious of moving more quietly now she knew the rebels were across the water, waiting for them.

As they walked, Jessica counted the different species of plants around her. For the first time, the rainforest felt menacing. She didn't let herself believe the malevolence surrounding her. The oppressive atmosphere was a trick of her mind, caused by the intense humidity, and knowing the rebels were so close and the jungle was so deadly. But no matter what logical reason she gave herself, it didn't stop fear from slithering down her spine.

At least there were no snakes. None that she could see, anyway.

To distract herself, she practiced the sign language letters and numbers Mike had taught her. She did them again and again until they were like second nature to her. She spelled her name a few times, then Mike's, until it was second nature.

About twenty minutes later, Mike stopped and turned to her with a grin. "Look," he pointed, and Jessica peered through the trees. "I think that's another bridge a bit farther up."

"Really?" Jessica asked, his excitement infectious, the strange foreboding from earlier instantly disappearing. She looked closer, finally seeing the hint of rope he was pointing at. "Thank God," she breathed.

They crept closer, and Mike pulled away to peer across the river.

"Are there rebels on that side?" she hissed.

"Not that I can see," he said, coming back to her side. "They must believe no one in their right mind would use this bridge when they have a perfectly good one back that way. And they'd be right, if we hadn't spotted them waiting for us in the shadows."

"Or maybe the bridge is unusable?"

"We won't know until we test it. But to do that we'll have to climb. Probably tonight, so the rebels don't catch sight of us."

Jessica stared up—and up. "Climb?" It hadn't occurred to her that climbing would be the only way to reach the bridge. She moved forward to get a better view, parting the lush undergrowth near the water.

The bridge was tied halfway up two trees on either side of the river, about seventy feet in the air. It was made of rope and planks of wood, like something out of a b-movie or a video game. Even from her vantage, the rope look frayed and green with moss, and a number of the boards were missing, having long ago broken off and fallen into the river below.

She glanced back the way they'd come, where she could see hints of the solid bridge through the trees. The bridge where the rebels were waiting to ambush them. She sighed wistfully. Though there was no way she'd risk crossing it, *that* bridge was so temptingly sturdy. It had obviously been built to withstand the rising river water, and wasn't nearly so far above ground level as the one hanging precariously above them.

"Why is it up so high?" she moaned.

"They must have put it up that high so it wouldn't get washed away in the flood, since they'd have to rebuild after every rainy season."

She returned her gaze to the bridge Mike intended them to cross. "It's so high," she said in a small voice.

"Yeah. But you're not afraid of heights. Right?"

"Right," she said, unconvincingly. She wasn't, not like she was afraid of snakes. But she still wasn't exactly confident climbing that high onto a death trap of a bridge, above what Mike claimed were crocodile-and-piranha infested waters.

"Is this the only way?" she asked, searching his face for a sign he held something back.

"Yes. But it'll be okay. Hopefully."

"That doesn't give me a great deal of confidence," she protested.

"I don't want to lie to you," Mike told her.

"I want the lie. Tell me the lie."

Mike hesitated. Then, after a second, he stepped forward and gripped her hands. He stared straight into her eyes, and for a second Jessica forgot what she had to be afraid of.

"It'll be fine," Mike stated, voice firm. His gaze never wavered from hers.

"Wow," Jessica breathed, as her heart somersaulted in her chest. "You're a really good liar."

"You know how I know it'll be okay?"

She shook her head.

"Because I won't let anything happen to you. No matter what."

Warmth filled her at his words. Her heart beat double time as she continued to stare into his eyes.

That was a hell of a thing for him to say. Particularly here and now, when she couldn't do anything about it.

"Okay," she said, having no idea where the sudden burst of confidence came from, but knowing it had something to do with Mike.

"We'll wait until tonight. Unfortunately, this bridge is in full view of where the rebels are waiting for us. Hopefully they won't think to look up, but we give ourselves a better chance if we go in the dark."

"What happens if they see us in the moonlight? It's pretty strong out here."

"It took us about twenty minutes to reach here from the other bridge. Presumably it will take them a little less. That still gives us both enough time to cross the river and then disappear into the rainforest."

Jessica eyed the bridge with trepidation. "We don't have much of a choice, do we?" she asked.

"Not really. Not good ones." He held up his hand to count off the numbers. "One, keep going and simply hope we find another bridge, one that's sturdier and out of view. Two, swim across the river only to most likely get swept downstream and eaten by something. Or three, cross the bridge and confront the rebels head on."

Jessica straightened her spine. He was right, this was the best option. As dangerous as it was, staying in the rainforest would be more so in the long run.

"Okay," she said, infusing as much confidence and determination into her voice as possible. "I know we were lucky to find this bridge at all, so I'm game."

Mike grinned at her. "That's my girl."

Warmth washed over her at the words. Mike was proud of her, and that meant more than she could have imagined.

They settled in to wait for the early hours of the morning. No fire this time, in case the rebels saw the smoke. Not that they needed it for heat. But it also meant they couldn't boil water to replenish Mike's canteen, or ward off the creatures determined to land on them now they were still. Jessica hoped none of them carried any nasty diseases, and that Mike's insect repellent was doing the trick.

Once it grew dark, they didn't even have conversation to entertain them, since Mike couldn't see her. Barely enough moonlight filtered through the dense canopy for her to see Mike's shape and know she wasn't alone. No one had told her the waiting—the terrible anticipation—was the worst part of a mission. Knowing what was coming and having the tension build and build until she was a bundle of nerves with no outlet.

Again she cycled through the sign language she knew, taking comfort in the repetition.

Finally, after hours of waiting, Mike leaned forward and gripped her shoulder. It was time.

Slowly, carefully, they ascended to the bridge. Jessica struggled without Mike's upper body strength, falling behind a few times. Mike noticed and slowed each time, but Jessica's stamina quickly waned.

She was panting by the time she squeezed herself through the last of the branches to sit heavily opposite Mike. She determinedly didn't look down, not wanting to know how bad the fall would be if she slipped. The moonlight was stronger here, without the trees and leaves blocking its path, enough for her to see Mike clearly. Instead of thinking of the drop below, she focused on Mike's face. His gaze was steady and he wasn't even breathing heavily. Bastard.

"I'll go first," he told her. "That way, if the bridge isn't stable, I'll be the one to fall."

Jessica blanched. "You think you'll fall?"

"No, but better me than you."

"Then what the hell would happen to me?"

"If I die—" He ignored her sound of protest. "I want you to go back to the rebels and turn yourself in."

"*What?*" she hissed.

"Hear me out. They want you alive. You're no good to them dead. You have a better chance of survival if you're with them instead of alone in the jungle, right? It'll give Soldiering On more time to send someone else to rescue you."

"Mike, if there's any chance you'll die crossing that bridge, don't do it. Please."

Her heart pounded. His words drilled deep into the fear center of her mind, clamping a vice around her lungs. She didn't want a contingency plan, couldn't bear to think of it. She wanted him alive and safe.

"We gotta cross," he said firmly. "It should be fine."

"I don't believe you."

He grinned, his usual picture of fearlessness. How did he do it? Why did he never freak out?

"I know," he told her. "But we have a better chance of surviving this than crossing through the river, or walking into an ambush. Those aren't bad odds."

"Mike—"

He gripped the back of her neck and pulled her forward into a kiss, cutting off her words. Jessica froze in shock. What the hell was he doing? But after a second, she didn't even care. She kissed him back just as fiercely, even as her fingers locked tighter on the branch she sat on.

The kiss lasted barely a second before Mike pulled away, determination etched on his features. Jessica nearly yanked him back to her before remembering where they were. She didn't want to overbalance him.

He stood and tested the first plank, keeping his weight on his back foot.

Jessica clambered to her feet, heart in her throat, as Mike transferred his weight to his front foot. The bridge groaned and shifted, the sound echoing down the river in the still night, and Jessica hoped it didn't reach the rebels. But the plank didn't instantly collapse, and Jessica breathed a sigh of relief. First hurdle jumped.

He stepped forward, keeping his steps light. He ran his hands over the ropes on either side, but didn't grip them. Smart move, since Jessica was convinced they'd rot to nothing at the slightest touch. How long had this bridge been here? Decades, at least.

Mike kept moving forward. Jessica's eyes riveted on his feet as she silently pleaded for him to make it across safely. Every now and again he had to take a larger step to skip a broken board or two, and the bridge would rock, making Jessica freeze in terror for him.

She kept half an ear out for a shout from below. They had to hope the rebels wouldn't bother looking up, but it was impossible to know. They could be waiting for Mike on the other side at this very moment.

About two-thirds of the way across, he paused. Jessica's only indication something was wrong was an ominous creaking, but Mike clearly sensed something wrong. He quickened his pace, moving across the remainder of the bridge at the speed of a walk instead of a crawl. As he neared the end, one of the boards cracked beneath his feet, tripping him. He gripped the ropes that passed for handrails to stop himself falling.

Jessica's fingers dug into the bark of the tree where she gripped its trunk, her eyes fixed on Mike and her heart in her throat.

The rope on the right snapped under his weight, making the whole bridge shudder. *Cross the last bit. Get to safety.* She clamped her jaw shut to stop herself saying it aloud.

The rope dangled useless in his hand, so Mike dropped it. He eased his foot up from the cracked board and tested the one ahead of it. Apparently it must have been safe, because he eased his foot down and then resumed the crossing. Jessica nearly cheered in relief as he finished the remaining few steps to the sturdy tree beyond.

Until she remembered it was her turn now, and the blood drained from her cheeks. She had to do what Mike had done, but with fewer boards and only one handrail.

She swallowed, fear making her hands tremble. More than anything, she wished she could stay exactly where she was. But Mike beckoned her from across the river, and she had to move.

She kept her eyes focused on Mike as she maneuvered herself into position at the start of the bridge. Then, she looked down at her feet. Her head spun as her eyes focused on the dizzying height below her.

Water, glinting with moonlight, rushed beneath her. She squeezed her eyes shut and swallowed, willing her heart to calm. When she was in control of herself again, she eased her eyes open. This time, she determinedly focused on the boards beneath her feet, not the rushing river beyond.

She loosened her fierce grip on the rope to her left and took a tentative step forward, and then another. She kept her mind focused on that—one foot in front of the other.

It wasn't until she was halfway across that something shocked her out of her focus. The bridge groaned and dropped. Jessica's eyes snapped up to see the rope she clutched unraveling at the other end, right next to Mike. Their gazes met—briefly—until he lunged to grab the rope to keep her steady. The rope slid through his grip and slithered off the side of the bridge to hang uselessly below.

Mike winced and gripped his hand. Sympathy and worry swelled within her, suspecting he'd have rope burns on his palms.

But then the true horror of her own situation penetrated her mind, and all the hair froze in her lungs. Now she stood high above the earth, with no barrier between her and a seventy-foot drop.

"You can do it, Jessica," came Mike's quiet whisper.

She glanced up to meet his gaze, still frozen.

"I can't come out to get you." His voice barely carried. "Our combined weight will probably break it. But you have to keep moving, sweetheart."

The endearment burrowed into her mind, but she couldn't think about it. Mike made an effort to keep his voice calm, though there was a slight tremble beneath the words. A second later, Jessica saw why. Beside him, the rope that held the bottom part of the bridge to the tree sagged, indicating it would snap any moment.

Jessica took a big breath, and then another. She had to move.

She forced her cramping fingers to release the useless rope that she still clutched, as if it was doing anything to protect her. She didn't watch it fall, too scared of catching a glimpse of the drop beneath her.

She stepped forward, putting as little of her weight on the bridge as possible. Even still, it dipped alarmingly, and Jessica didn't have much time. She was torn between making a break for the end, and continuing slowly to put as little stress as possible on the crumbling bridge.

Her gaze bounced between her feet, the fraying rope, and Mike's worried expression.

Nearly there. A few more steps and she'd be safe.

But the rope gave way, snapping until only a fragile twist held the bridge to the tree, the broken strands unraveling at the speed of a bullet. Jessica didn't think. She put her head down and sprinted forward, launching herself at Mike the same second the rope snapped for good. He snatched her out of the air and into his arms as the bridge collapsed beneath her, still dangling from the tree by one frayed rope.

Mike pulled her close as her boots found a tree branch to steady herself. He wrapped one arm around the tree trunk to steady them, and flattened his other against her lower back to press her closer to him.

Her heart pounded like it was trying to break out of her chest and the cold sweat that had formed on her skin chilled her despite the humidity. She buried her face in Mike's shoulder and breathed hard, calming herself.

She'd survived. They both had. Being alive was the only thing that mattered.

As her heart rate calmed, she became more aware of Mike's body against hers. Their mingled heartbeats, the splay of his hand against her back, the soft exhalation of breaths on her shoulder.

"Thank God you're all right," he murmured, pulling her even closer.

He'd kissed her.

She hadn't thought about it at all during her daring flight over the bridge, but he *had* kissed her. Too quickly. She hadn't even had a chance to enjoy it.

Her body stiffened, and he pulled back to see her face.

"You okay?"

She nodded, unable to speak.

"Then let's get back to solid ground."

She swallowed at the reminder of how high up they were, but was immediately desperate to get to solid ground, get safe.

They shimmied down, taking their time. Jessica's arms ached from the climb up on the other side of the river, but thankfully gravity did most of the work on the descent.

Jessica still half-expected the rebels would be waiting for them at the bottom. But when they finally caught sight of the moist ground, it appeared empty. Mike dropped down first and took off his pack to stretch briefly, then held his arms up for Jessica.

She lowered herself, but her arms unexpectedly gave out. She collapsed into Mike's arms harder than she'd intended, sending them both to the forest floor. Mike landing on his back with Jessica on top of him. Her breasts were crushed against his chest, their lips scant inches away.

"Sorry," Jessica breathed. Their gazes met. The world stilled.

"I'm not," replied Mike. And then he kissed her again.

This wasn't the quick, firm kiss from before. This was slow and wet and sensual. He coaxed her mouth open and slid his tongue inside. Jessica fisted his shirt and teased his tongue with her own. The taste of papaya and wood smoke overwhelmed her senses as she deepened the kiss.

Mike cupped her head, fingers tangling in her hair, and explored her mouth with an exquisite unhurriedness.

But her heart still pounded from the adrenaline that had flooded her system earlier, and unhurried was *not* what she wanted. She kissed him harder, maneuvering her mouth to get the best angle. Mike didn't complain about the change in pace, matching each stroke of her tongue with his own.

He groaned, and the sound sent tugs of pleasure down to her clit. She threaded her fingers through his hair and tightened her grip. In response, his hand slipped over her ass and squeezed.

Jessica gasped, breaking the kiss, and Mike had the chance to move his lips to her neck. He placed hot, open-mouthed kisses against the sensitive skin, and Jessica's hips flexed in want. Friction. She wanted friction.

Mike's hand slipped farther, reaching between her legs until he could rub his fingers over the seam of her crotch. It wasn't enough, not nearly enough.

She shifted, brushing her breasts against his chest in the process. It made her nipples stand to attention, begging for his touch as much of the rest of her.

He returned his mouth to hers, as he found her clit, circling it until she panted with want. Shit, she was going to come right here, in the middle of the goddamn jungle. This hadn't been how she'd imagined this would happen, but she sure as hell wasn't complaining.

She was already so close, so ready and—

Mike pushed her off him with a bit of curse.

"What the hell?" Jessica asked, anger surging. If he thought he could cop a feel and then not finish what he'd started, he was in for a rude shock.

"Stay back." He sat up, wincing.

"What, so you can go on some guilt trip and say you regret what happened? Fuck that."

"No," he gritted out. "There's a slight issue."

His jaw was locked tight. The pained expression on his face gave her pause. "What?" she asked. If he apologized for that kiss, so help her, she'd kick him in the nuts again.

He stood and turned his back to her. Jessica followed him into a standing position, ready to call him out for his rudeness. But then he reached behind him and tugged up his shirt.

On his back, latched onto his skin, were five fat leeches, happily sucking his blood.

CHAPTER NINE

Mike turned back to Jessica, biting back a curse. The leeches had chosen the worst possible time to interrupt. The rebels were minutes down the river, and he'd finally had Jessica in his arms. She'd been so hot, so demanding, and his cock was still aching from the memory of her against him.

He wanted her there again. But not on a forest floor this time. A bed. Or a hammock, he wasn't fussy. But definitely somewhere comfortable, where they wouldn't be interrupted. They needed to finish their intimate moment, without the leeches this time.

No doubt that would stop the strange thrum in his chest whenever he thought of her. A little voice in his head called him a liar, but he ignored it. He wasn't built for relationships, but sex he could do. Happily. Particularly when it came to a woman like Jessica.

Christ, she was sexy. Her breasts alone…well, he regretted not getting his hands on those a second ago when he'd had the chance.

The pain in his back intensified, reminding him that now was not the time for sex fantasies. He needed to get the bloodsuckers off his back. They weren't lethal, not right away, but they could definitely cause some damage.

Jessica crouched. Mike almost asked what she was doing, but it was too dark for him to see her answer, anyway, now they weren't inches away. She stuck a hand in his pack and eventually extracted something. A second later his flashlight clicked on, and Jessica pointed it at her lips.

"Tell me what to do. Do I pull them off?"

He grinned, oddly warmed by her forethought of grabbing the flashlight, so he didn't have to ask. He tore off his shirt and placed it on top of the pack, so he wouldn't get any nasties crawling in it in the dark.

"No, don't pull them off. Their fangs can get stuck under the skin. We need either citrus fruit, or matches. Since I don't have many matches left, let's try for the citrus."

"You're very calm," Jessica said. She let the light linger on his chest for a few seconds, her gaze heating, then swung the beam around to search the trees.

"Leeches aren't deadly. They don't carry diseases or anything. The only thing to worry about is if the wounds bleed a lot, since they have an anticoagulant in their saliva. I'm a long way from blood loss."

She nodded, and then the beam of the flashlight stopped on a cluster of guavas. She gathered a couple and brought them back to him. Mike cut them open and she squeezed them on his back. He barely noticed the sensation, but the scent was potent. Until he got a proper wash, his back would be sticky with juice and blood.

Jessica came around to where he could see her.

"All gone?" he asked.

She shook her head and aimed the light at her face. "You had five of them. I've got rid of three. But the other two aren't responding to the guava."

He sighed. "Damn. I hoped it would be tart enough, but obviously not. We need a lemon or lime."

Jessica glanced around as if one might fall from the sky, but no miracle occurred.

"So, you want me to burn them off?"

"May as well. Don't waste too many matches," he told her.

She narrowed her eyes at him, then dropped the beam so he couldn't read her face. He grinned again, liking her spirit.

Once she had the matches out of the pack, he turned back around. He flinched a little at the first touch of flame, since it was unexpected. After that, he held still as Jessica burned the leeches until they shriveled.

Finally, the heat disappeared, and Jessica came into view.

"Three matches down," she said proudly.

"Nice work."

"So—" She broke off, her eyes darting over his shoulder and into the darkness.

He dropped his voice and leaned forward until he could press his lips against her ear.

"What is it?"

Jessica pulled back and aimed the light at her face. "I heard a shout." She mouthed it soundlessly, he could tell by the way her throat worked.

"They must have seen the light. Or the broken bridge, and figured out what happened. We have to go," he breathed. "How close were they?"

"I think they're only leaving now."

"Good. Then we'll have a twenty-minute head start."

Mike threw his shirt back on and then picked up the pack. He took the flashlight from Jessica and clicked it off. He'd have to navigate by what little moonlight penetrated the canopy. He couldn't risk the rebels seeing the light and knowing how to follow them.

They moved through the dark, deeper and deeper into the blackness until they could only see the vaguest outlines of plants and trees. They were slow, careful, not wanting to walk into anything they shouldn't.

Mike didn't know whether it would be safer to stop and wait for morning, or whether to keep plowing through the forest with no indication he headed the right way. He hated the lack of sight, added to his lack of hearing. It made him—and therefore, Jessica—increasingly vulnerable.

He had no idea if anyone was following them, but since Jessica hadn't reacted, he presumed there weren't any sounds of pursuit. They must have escaped just in time.

Eventually, they'd have to stop. Jessica was slowing, and Mike was suffering the effects of a sleepless night himself. A little farther, and then they could make camp.

An hour before dawn, Jessica grabbed Mike from behind and pushed him against a tree, clapping her hand over his mouth. His cock stood to attention before his brain registered what she was doing. He stilled, struggling to focus with her body pressed against his.

His head was still full of their earlier kiss, his body desperate to finish what they'd started. That was the only excuse he could give when it took him a solid minute to see the lights filtering through the undergrowth.

He squinted, peering closer, trying to make sense of what was in front of him. The rebels shouldn't have been able to circle around that fast. He and Jessica had been heading in a mostly-straight line since the river. Unless he'd somehow got turned around in the dark? But, no, being deaf shouldn't have messed with his sense of direction. Not that much, anyway.

Jesus, he wished he could hear. It would give him way more context to what he saw. He dared not ask Jessica. Not when she still had her hand clamped over his mouth to silence him.

Were the rebels nearby?

The lights brightened. Wait, no. They were moving, coming closer. The ground beneath his feet vibrated. He held his breath, heart pounding and muscles tensed for a fight. The lights reached a crescendo of brightness, filling the entire clearing like sunlight.

Mike met Jessica's gaze, and their eyes locked. He couldn't read her expression. Concern was there, but also something more.

But then, the lights moved past, slowly dimming until there was nothing but blackness surrounding them once again. Mike didn't move, letting his eyes adjust to the darkness once again. Jessica stayed pressed against him, breathing hard.

He settled his hands on her hips, relishing the contact between them. If she moved her hand from his mouth he could—

She stepped back, and his arms instantly felt empty without her in them.

A shift in the air told him she was moving, and then the flashlight clicked on.

"Are you sure that's safe?" he asked urgently.

She nodded. "The trucks are gone. I haven't heard the rebels for a few hours. I think we've lost them."

Mike breathed a sigh of relief. "Trucks?"

"I think that's what they were."

"Huh. I doubt that road is on any map."

"Should we check it out?"

He agreed, so they crept forward in the direction the lights had come from. Moments later, they stood on the edge of what passed for a road. It was barely as wide as a truck would be. The ground hadn't even been cleared properly. More like the trucks had driven over the soil and undergrowth to flatten it.

Mike wasn't surprised. From what he knew about loggers, they moved locations and paths often, and kept their operations on the down-low. Neither of those things meant taking the time to clear a proper road through the jungle was a good use of their time.

Not that the Zolegan government would cause trouble for the loggers, provided they got enough kickbacks. But given rebel activity in the area, it was a smart enough move for these loggers to avoid drawing unnecessary attention to themselves.

"Should we follow it?" Jessica asked when he looked at her.

Mike shook his head. "It's going in the wrong direction. And it'll make us easier to spot if the rebels are still on our tail."

She nodded. "Okay. So, we keep walking?"

Exhaustion was etched beneath her eyes. Her shoulders slumped, but her expression was determined. Mike wanted nothing more than to tell her she could take a break. It wasn't long before dawn, and they'd need to get some rest if they were to continue once daylight hit.

But he couldn't. Not here, not now. They were far too close to the road. And while the loggers were a better option than the rebels, there was no guarantee they'd let Mike and Jessica continue their journey with safe passage. Not when they knew the two of them could spill the beans on their illegal activities.

"We have to walk a bit farther to get away from the road and anyone that might see us. Then we'll grab a few hours' sleep."

She nodded, and pride swelled in his chest. She really was brave, and resilient. She hadn't freaked out or squirmed over the leeches, she hadn't lost her nerve on the bridge. She didn't complain now, when he was asking her to do something he'd hesitate to request of any of his highly-trained colleagues.

Jessica Vanderslice was a surprising and remarkable woman. Everything he'd expected from her had been so far from the truth.

He'd never been more glad of a person exceeding all his expectations. If he'd been trapped in the jungle with the high-maintenance socialite he'd expected, this whole trip would have been a nightmare.

But then again, if he *had* been trapped with an awful woman, he wouldn't be dealing with these new feelings he wasn't quite sure what to do with.

He sighed and shook off the thought.

He and Jessica crossed the logging road, and then plunged back into the dark forest.

Mike finally called a halt to their progress as dawn filtered through the trees. Jessica collapsed back onto a tree trunk and gave him a grateful smile. They set up the camp, hanging the hammocks. Mike debated whether he should light a fire to keep away bugs and boil some water, but eventually decided against it. It would be easier for the rebels to spot the smoke in the daytime.

Jessica fell instantly asleep with her night t-shirt over her face to block out the light. Mike lay back in his hammock and forced himself to follow her lead. He needed the rest. But instead his head was filled with Jessica, and the way she'd pressed against him. He wanted her. More than he'd wanted a woman in a long time. Maybe ever. It wasn't only her beauty that drew him, but her courage and determination, too.

It had to be the close proximity. Once they were out of the jungle, away from the sultry heat and adrenaline caused by running for their lives, it would all go away. It had to. Because what the hell kind of life could a man like him have with a senator's daughter?

None.

He pictured her, standing with a serene beauty behind her mother on the campaign trail, the only image he'd had of her before rescuing her from that camp. She was so controlled and untouchable. He tried to insert himself into the image, but drew a blank. That kind of thing wasn't for him. The senator would want him far away from her next campaign, and fair enough, too.

There was no future for him and Jessica. He had nothing to offer her. Not that he wanted anything long-term, hadn't considered it since returning to US soil after his final tour. His eyes darted to his pack, where the coin he carried was nestled in an interior pocket. His lucky charm. He scoffed at the thought.

Yeah, he definitely didn't want to get too attached to anyone. Attachments led to pain, he'd learned that the hard way.

His gaze rose from his pack, only to lock onto Jessica's. She was wide awake and staring right at him.

"You should sleep," he said.

She gave him a tired smile. "Can't settle. Too sore. And the light." She pointed up to illustrate her point. The sunlight hit her right in the face, keeping her awake even with the t-shirt acting as an eye mask.

"You should try, anyway. Even if you don't sleep, the rest will do your body good."

She shrugged and shifted in her hammock, facing him. "Tell me a bedtime story."

Mike frowned, wondering if he'd read her lips right. Then, he understood. He turned his body towards her. Since he hadn't built a fire, their hammocks were closer than usual, and he could read her lips easily enough in the burgeoning light.

"What kind of story?" he asked.

"Tell me about the coin." Her face was soft, and he imagined her voice would imply a gentle suggestion. But he tensed anyway, his mind shying away from the idea.

"You don't have to," she said, waving her hands. "Forget I said anything."

Mike took a deep breath. "No, it's okay. It's not really a secret. I just don't like talking about it."

Jessica nodded, but she didn't interrupt.

"I had this buddy. Ramirez. We were on the same team." He paused. "The coin was his."

Jessica curled her arm beneath her head and watched him steadily.

"It was his lucky coin. He'd won it in a poker game years ago, and from then on, he took it with him wherever he went. If he had a narrow escape, he would always say it was the coin that saved him. I think it might've been a joke at first, but he soon believed it. Wouldn't go anywhere without it."

An ache started behind Mike's eyes. It had been a long time since he'd remembered Ramirez in this much detail.

"I was sent on a mission. A dangerous one. Ramirez gave me the coin, to protect me." Mike sent Jessica a wry smile.

"What happened?" she asked.

"The base was attacked while I was gone. He…he didn't make it."

Tears blurred Jessica's eyes, and she leaned out of her hammock to grip his hand. "I'm so sorry," she told him.

Mike nodded and squeezed her hand in return. He was sorry, too. Ramirez was a good man. And even though Mike wasn't superstitious, he couldn't help but think if his friend had had his lucky coin that day, he'd still be here now.

"I didn't find out until much later. That was my last mission. The one that lost me my hearing." That whole time had been a total clusterfuck of grief and guilt and loss. He still couldn't think of it without simmering rage and pain.

"That must have been awful." Jessica's gaze didn't hold pity, thank God.

"It was. Believe me. If I'd known, I never would've taken the coin. He kept insisting." He shrugged, but that familiar misery swept over him again.

Jessica tightened her hand in his, anchoring him. "You couldn't know ahead of time what would happen."

"I thought it was a silly superstition he had. That I'd get the coin back to him in a few days, and he'd be fine in the meantime." He hadn't believed in the power of the coin. He still wasn't sure he did. But Mike couldn't help thinking *what if…*

"It might have been a superstition. There are too many factors in something like that to attribute it to a lucky coin."

Mike pressed his lips into a line. He'd told himself the same thing hundreds of times, but it never stuck. "Even so, his belief in it might have saved him if he'd had it."

"And maybe that one change would've meant you died, instead." Her eyes glistened at the words.

"That would have been better," Mike gritted out. "He had a wife, and a kid."

"That's sad," she said, swallowing heavily. "But it doesn't mean your life is worth nothing." Jessica's expression was fierce, and a reluctant smile curved Mike's lips.

"I just…I think about it a lot. The chances of fate. It's not something I ever believed in before going to war." He rubbed an absent thumb over the back of her hand.

"Fate?" she asked, and he nodded. "I think about that sometimes, too. How different my life would have been if I'd made different choices. The little moments along the way that sent me in one direction or the other. Or was I always meant to do this one thing I've chosen? It's impossible to know for sure."

"I suppose it comforts people to put it all down to fate," he mused. "They don't have to worry they made the wrong choice, because it was fate they make *that* one."

"Sounds more like wanting to absolve responsibility for their actions," she said, twisting her mouth into a grumpy line. Mike grinned, the pain in his chest easing somewhat at the involuntary action. She was such an interesting mix of heart and fire. She had so much empathy for people, but she still wanted to hold them accountable for their actions—him included. It was refreshing and admirable.

"So, you keep the coin for luck?" she asked, turning the conversation back to its original purpose.

It would have been easy to say yes. To ignore the real reason he dragged that coin around like a weight on his back. She'd believe him, and then he could stop talking about it. But something about Jessica made him want to tell her the truth.

"I keep it to remind me of Ramirez, and of the debt I owe him. I came back from my mission alive, and he didn't."

"That's not your fault, Mike."

Death happened in war. It was unavoidable. But that didn't stop him from blaming himself for Ramirez. He never should have taken that coin from his friend.

Jessica squeezed his hand, recapturing the attention he'd let drift.

"Think of it this way. From the sounds of things, you and Ramirez were close, right?"

Mike nodded cautiously.

"If it had been your lucky coin, and you believed it had the power to save one person, what would you have done with it? Kept it for yourself? Or given it to Ramirez?"

Mike stared at her, his heart pounding as a lump formed in his throat. "Given it to him." He didn't have to think about the answer, it was immediate and right.

"Do you think Ramirez would have done the same for you?"

Mike swallowed. "Yeah." In fact, Mike knew he would have. That's what you did for your brother, your closest friend.

Jessica didn't say any more. She didn't have to. Her point had been elegantly made. The guilt he'd been carrying with him along with the coin eased slightly, allowing him to breathe for the first time in a long while.

He lay there, staring up at the light filtering through the canopy, his fingers entangled with Jessica's as he contemplated this new way of seeing things. By the time he looked back at Jessica, she was deeply asleep.

And soon Mike was, too.

CHAPTER TEN

It was the noise that reached her, first. A violent crushing and grinding that was unlike anything she'd ever heard before.

She put a hand on Mike's arm to alert him, but she had no way of describing what she was hearing, so she gave up and shrugged in defeat. The two of them moved forward cautiously until the trees fell away.

Beyond them was a huge open space, marked by tree stumps. Hundreds of them. Giant trucks holding logs at least ten times the size of Jessica hovered near the road, while cranes bigger than she'd ever seen lifted more on top of the stack.

The rainforest, so beautiful and pristine, was utterly decimated.

Loggers.

She and Mike hid behind some ferns, watching the activity on the far side of the clearing. This must have been where the trucks they'd heard had come from.

Jessica's heart broke. All the untouched wildness of the place had been destroyed for profit by these people. It was this kind of thing that harmed indigenous communities, and put the rest of the world in danger. The trees in the Amazon also helped eat huge amounts of the carbon dioxide in the atmosphere, a win for the entire world. She'd done enough fundraisers for charities protecting the rainforest that she knew how devastating logging could be.

But the corrupt government of Zolego didn't care about any of that. They only cared about the under-the-table profits they could get from the loggers. Jessica had spent some time protesting and organizing against the loggers in Zolego and the surrounding countries, and she knew how they got away with it. All they needed was some forged paperwork and they could claim the wood they collected from this protected area was actually from the legal logging area somewhere else. Once the wood went into the processing plants, it essentially became invisible, since there was no way to tell where it had come from.

There were legal protections in place to stop this from happening. But in Zolego they were mostly for show, since the government agencies did nothing to uphold their own laws. It made Jessica utterly furious.

"They shouldn't be here," she hissed. She turned to Mike, but he wasn't looking at her. He stared over the cleared area, a frown on his face.

Jessica nudged him with her shoulder and he glanced over. "Hmmm?"

"They shouldn't be here."

"I know."

"We have to do something."

His frown darkened. "No. No way. What can we do against this whole operation?"

"I don't know," she hissed. "You're always the one with a plan. All I know is we can't let them get away with this."

"We have to," he said firmly. "I'm not putting you at risk to sabotage such a massive operation. Particularly not with no plan, back up, or resources."

"But, Mike—"

He cut her off with a frustrated shake of his head. "I know you want to help. I get it. This charity stuff, protecting others, it's second nature to you. But this time, there isn't anything you can do."

Jessica set her jaw, mutinous.

"Jessica, please. You can protest all you want once I have you safely back in the US. I don't care what you do after that. But I promised I'd bring you home safely to your parents, and I won't let anything stand in my way. Not even you."

The urge to argue welled up within her, but she tamped it down. He was right. There wasn't really anything they could do right now, no matter how much she might want to. Two people—even if one was a highly trained operative—could do little against the forty or so people in the clearing. They'd most likely be caught, and if they weren't killed on sight, they could be turned over to the rebels. The worst she and Mike could do was maybe slow them down for a day, but that would hardly hurt them, not in the long run. Better to keep herself safe now so that she could do more damage later, once she was back stateside. She had enough contacts from her charity work and protests that she was sure she could find someone who had the power to shut this place down once and for all.

She couldn't risk being recaptured by the rebels. Not for herself, since Mike had already pointed out that they wanted her alive. But she could easily imagine them hurting Mike, even killing him since he held no value to them, and that was something she couldn't allow.

"Fine," she said, and Mike nodded in satisfaction.

"We'll need to go around the clearing." He sighed. "It'll add another half day to our trek."

Jessica stared at him for a long moment, and then around the clearing. He was right. The area was so large that it would take them most of the day to circle around it.

"We won't ever get out of here," she lamented on a sigh. "Like we're on a treadmill, fixed in place."

Mike grinned. "We'll get out. It's slow progress, but I promise we'll get there."

She gave him a smile to show she appreciated his effort, but inside her heart sank. She wanted to be home, and showered, and eating something that wasn't parrot or fruit.

"Is there some way we can make up the time?" she asked. She didn't want to be out here any longer than necessary.

Would her parents be worried about her? Surely Mike's colleague, Charlie, had told everyone what had happened at the airport. But it had now been nearly a week since anyone had heard from her or Mike. She hoped Charlie would wait for them. Mike seemed confident he would, so she had to trust that.

And if not, then she'd rely on Mike to get her home safe, anyway. He had a backup plan and contingency for everything. He hadn't been frustrated, or ruffled, by anything the rebels or this rainforest had thrown their way. It really was incredible.

"I don't think we can—" He paused, cutting himself off. His gaze shifted to the trucks and a speculative look crossed his face.

She nudged him. "What is it?"

"Well, the road we crossed headed the wrong way, back closer to the city, right?"

"Right," she agreed.

"But look at that truck." He pointed to one easing out of the clearing now. It took her a full minute to understand what Mike had. The truck turned left, away from them. It would head in the opposite direction to the one they'd come from.

Jessica's eyes went wide. "It's going the right way," she said, excitement fusing her voice. "Why are they heading towards the border?"

Mike shrugged. "They might have multiple processing plants. Or, if we're lucky, they're sneaking wood into another country. Then, they won't have to claim it on their forms and there'll be no record of it."

"So it's possible we can take the truck all the way to Colombia? That would save us days!"

Mike gripped her wrist. "Don't get too excited. It's a risk, because we don't know exactly where the road goes. It could loop back around. We also need to figure out how to get on the truck undetected."

"I don't care. Finally, something is going right. I fully intend to be excited about it."

He grinned and chuckled. "Fine. But don't blame me if it turns out to be a disappointment."

"I won't."

They skirted the edge of the clearing. It took hours to reach where the action was, since once they got close they had to fight through the undergrowth without the use of the kukri blade. They didn't want to draw attention to themselves by sight or sound.

The sun began its descent beneath the horizon, sending a golden glow across the clearing. Darkness loomed, and that would be the perfect time to sneak aboard one of the vehicles.

The huge trucks loomed above them, stacked high with tree trunks, blocking the view of the action. They were secured using heavy chains so they wouldn't slip during transport. Jessica suspected they were filled higher than was safe, and wondered if illegal loggers followed any safety guidelines. Since the trucks had to travel long distances from the center of the Amazon to the processing plants, they would stack as much wood in the back as would fit to cut down on trips.

She studied the truck nearest to them. She couldn't immediately see a place to hide. Only the cab of the truck, where the driver would be, and the flatbed at the back where they'd put the tree trunks. There wasn't even a back seat to the truck's cab that they could sneak into. Clearly, the loggers used whatever space they could for the valuable wood.

She turned to Mike. "What's your plan?"

He twisted his face, showing he was thinking, and returned his gaze to the trucks. "We can't hide on top of the wood, we'll be seen. Can't hide underneath it, because we'll be squashed."

"So you don't think your plan will work?" Her heart sank. She wanted home more fiercely than she'd wanted anything.

"I'm not giving up yet."

"We could steal one?" she suggested, doubtfully. He'd shoot the idea down, but she had to try.

He shook his head. "Too risky. They'd catch up in no time. No way they wouldn't notice."

"Do they work through the night? Maybe we could wait for it to go dark and do it then?"

He shrugged. "Since they were on the road last night, they must have a twenty-four-hour operation. Probably cutting back the trees and loading them during the day, driving them to the plant and back at night. Or working in shifts, some day drivers, some night drivers."

"That makes sense." She sighed, exhaustion and misery lapping at her edges. "Shit."

He sent her a smile. "Don't give up yet."

"What more can we do? I can't see any place to hide on these trucks."

They circled around farther, still keeping the trucks in sight on their right but staying behind the tree line. Through a gap between two trucks, a group of men talked with bored expressions. All wore hard hats. One held a clipboard. Management? Behind them, a man waved his arms vigorously at a crane operator lifting one of the tree trunks. He stopped immediately when he caught sight of the man on the ground. Business as usual.

"How will we get past all these people?" Jessica asked. She had no doubt there were more men where she couldn't see them. This was a huge operation, and it wouldn't be easy to sneak by unnoticed.

"If we can get into the trucks from this side, we won't have to."

They kept walking, examining every truck they passed. The shadows deepened beneath the canopy.

They didn't dare get too close, in case they were spotted, so stuck to the safety of the undergrowth and darkness in the uncleared part of the rainforest. Jessica was rapidly running out of hope and excitement as the sun sunk behind the trees.

"That one," Mike said eventually, pointing. He swung his pack off his back and unstrapped the hammocks, ignoring Jessica's confused frown.

It took Jessica a moment to figure out why he'd singled out that truck. Then, she saw it. Between the cab of the truck and the wood being stacked behind it was a storage box. Little bigger than a coffin and made of steel, it would barely fit two people lying down if they squeezed.

She almost refused. Trapped in that box with no air, Mike pressed against her?

But then the truck turned on, its loud engine idling.

"It's leaving."

Mike glanced at the box, and then back at her. "No time to think. Let's do it." He swung the pack onto his back, leaving the hammocks behind.

They sprinted toward the truck, careful to keep out of sight of the workers nearby. But once they reached the truck, they had to stop. Since the box sat between the cab and the wood, it was visible from both sides. Anyone in the clearing who looked their way while they snuck inside would see them.

"What do we do?" she asked.

The truck rolled forward, slow and steady. Mike sent her an apologetic smile.

"We'll have to risk it. Be quick."

Without giving her time to think, to protest, he vaulted onto the truck and flung open the box. Jessica jogged beside the truck, keeping pace as it moved towards the exit.

Mike held out a hand for her. Jessica grabbed it, planted her foot on the truck bed, and allowed Mike to haul her up. He glanced around, then grabbed her hand and stuffed her into the thankfully-empty box. No shouts of warning reached her, but the truck's engine may have drowned them out.

Then, Mike took off his pack and leaped in beside her, spooning around her body. He placed the pack over their legs and then reached over to shut the lid. It didn't quite close, not with the pack sticking up above the sides of the box, but Jessica was grateful for that. It allowed light and air into the cramped space.

Jessica's heart thundered and she strained her ears for any sound. But there was nothing other than the heavy rumble of the truck and Mike's breath on the back of her neck.

For a long moment, she concentrated on slowing her heart rate as the truck picked up speed. She breathed deep and allowed herself to be grateful they'd managed to get away with that little stunt.

When nothing eventful happened for a long while, Jessica relaxed, her muscles loosening. She hadn't noticed how tense she'd been holding herself until she had a moment to breathe.

Exhaustion dragged at her. She'd spent the night trekking through the jungle, and had only managed a few hours' sleep that morning before Mike woke her to continue their journey. Now, they were in for a long drive, and Jessica didn't see any reason to stay awake for it. In the warmth and darkness, with Mike's comforting presence beside her, she drifted to sleep.

Mike shifted against her, and Jessica woke with a start. It took her a second to get her bearings before she remembered where they were. How long had she slept? She yawned as her body came awake, much more rested.

That's when Jessica noticed Mike's erection. There was nowhere to move in the cramped space, to pretend out of politeness she hadn't noticed. And, frankly, she didn't want to.

Excitement and renewed energy burst through her, focusing on Mike at her back. They couldn't talk—not with words—while only a thin stream of light penetrated the darkness of the box.

The truck hit a pothole, jerking them, and Mike's hand fell on her hip. He left it sitting there, burning a hole through her trousers.

Jessica moved, only a fraction, pressing herself more firmly against Mike's erection. He groaned, and he slid his hand around to splay against her stomach. It was a wordless test, asking her whether she wanted the same thing he did. Jessica's heart skittered. This was it. Point of no return. And she didn't want to turn back.

Some part of her knew she should. She shouldn't be considering having sex with a man when they were in such a perilous situation. But a little fun wouldn't hurt, right? She liked Mike, was attracted to him. They could spend some time naked together while on their adventure, and then go their separate ways once they were back on US soil. It wouldn't have to be anything more than that.

But a whisper at the corner of her mind told her she didn't want that. She liked Mike. Liked his bravery and competence. Liked that he always kept calm under pressure, and always had a plan. She wanted to know how that would translate into the real world, when doing normal things. Would he be the kind of man who always had a contingency plan if a night out didn't go as planned? She got the sense that he wouldn't yell at servers if they got his order wrong, or berate a cab driver if he went the wrong way. Was he as talented at everyday things as he was at surviving in the jungle? Jessica couldn't imagine he'd be anything other than spectacular with his fingers and mouth and cock. Not if the taste she'd had so far was a good indicator.

He'd be a good partner. A good partner for *her*, in such a way she'd never considered any man.

Jessica had traveled the world, doing good. She hadn't had the time or inclination to form real romantic ties with anyone. Inevitably, they'd want her to stay.

But with Mike? He was someone she'd consider coming home to. Someone she would stay for. Or someone she would invite to go with her on adventures. He'd spent time traveling, helping people, too. Maybe it was something they could do together?

She still had no plans for her future. She didn't know how she'd feel about her volunteer work once she was safely back home. Would she be willing to risk another kidnapping? Or would she prioritize her safety, and find another way to contribute to the world? How could she know, when everything was so unsettled?

But she was starting to think that whatever she decided, she wanted Mike to be a part of it. Some way, somehow. They'd shared too much to part now. Like they would forever be linked and intertwined because of this mad adventure they'd shared.

But she couldn't focus on that. There was plenty of time for that once she was home. For now, all she knew was that she wanted Mike, and she intended to have him.

She slid her hand over his, where it still rested on her stomach. Then, she pushed it up, over her shirt, until he cupped a breast. His breath hitched as he lightly squeezed, and Jessica felt both the sound and the sensation down to her core.

Mike's lips brushed the sensitive spot behind her ear. Jessica drew in a breath, already hot and wanting, when they'd even barely started. But she'd been ready for this since they'd met, her body primed to snap into action at the slightest hint. The kiss last night—had it really only been last night?—hadn't helped.

Mike was bolder now, sucking on her neck as he played with her breasts through her bra. Her breathing came out in heavy pants and her skin tightened in need. She wanted to touch him, but there wasn't much of him she could reach. They were so crammed in the box she couldn't even turn around.

She reached back to find his ass, encouraging him to press his erection harder into her butt.

He groaned again, hips flexing, and Jessica grinned in the darkness. He was so hard with need for her. It made her feel powerful and sensual even in a tiny steel box.

But it wasn't enough. Her clit ached, desperate for friction.

"Mike," she groaned, but he couldn't hear her.

Well, she'd just have to take matters into her own hands. Mike could only use one, after all.

Jessica unbuttoned her pants and slid the zipper down. She hooked her leg over Mike's to give herself room, shifting his pack in the process. She dipped her hand inside her underwear, brushing against her sensitive clit. Her internal walls clenched around nothing, and she wished more than anything Mike could slide his thick cock into her right now. Instead, she inserted a finger into her channel as she pressed the heel of her hand against her clit, easing the ache building there.

Mike still played with her breasts, planting hot kisses anywhere he could reach with his lips. His actions sent answering pulls to her core.

She slipped another finger inside herself, hips rotating at the sensation. Mike broke, growling and his hand disappeared from her breast. Jessica had a moment of confusion, but then he gripped her wrist and eased her hand away.

"Mine," he whispered into the low light. The deep rumble of his voice caused a shiver to run down her spine even as her skin heated.

His hand replaced hers. He played with her clit for a long moment, until she squirmed against his fingers. She used her now-free hand to play with her breasts as Mike dipped two fingers inside her, stretching her, filling her.

"Yes," she hissed. It wasn't as good as his cock, but she'd take it.

She tilted her knee up, giving him more room to work, and he murmured in approval. His lips returned to her neck, nibbling the sensitive skin, and Jessica knew she wasn't far from orgasm.

He worked his fingers in and out of her, in time with the kisses on her neck. The heel of his hand rubbed her clit and Jessica squirmed, torn between getting closer and farther away. He increased his pace, fucking her with his fingers until she could barely breathe. Her chest was tight, her skin burned.

And then she shattered, coming hard as he continued to pump his fingers into her. She pressed her mouth into her shoulder to muffle her cry as pleasure exploded through every inch of her. Mike rode out the contractions, not letting up until she was limp and exhausted in his arms. He extracted his hand, then placed a gentle kiss on her neck, soothing the over-sensitized skin.

Dimly, Jessica registered the truck slowing, but she didn't pay much attention. It had done so a few times already, presumably to turn corners easier. She was too focused on Mike. She wanted to return the favor he'd given her. He was still hard, his erection pressing into her back.

A tension ran through his body that she was desperate to ease. She reached a hand behind her to rub lazily against his cock, over his trousers. He shifted his hips, making it easier for her to reach.

She was so focused on Mike that she almost didn't notice the truck had stopped entirely. Not until Mike's head came up. Jessica froze. What the hell?

It was only then she heard the voices over the idling engine. They spoke Portuguese. The drivers? No there were at least three distinct voices.

Shit.

Jessica raised her hand into the weak light coming through the cracked lid, and made the symbol for three that Mike had taught her. Then, she pointed outside to indicate the men at the front.

"Fuck. We'll have to make a run for it." His voice was so low in her ear she barely heard it. But she nodded. The men out there were either rebels, or government officials, and either way Jessica didn't want to get caught. She hurriedly zipped and buttoned her pants.

"You'll have to make the call for when we run. When they're distracted, or out of view. But don't leave it too long."

Her heart pounded. Jesus. This wasn't her strength. This was Mike's area of expertise. How the hell was she supposed to know when was a good time to make a break for it? Panic thickened her throat. What if they caught her? She'd be tied up on that chair again, and who knew if she'd get free again. Oh God, oh God.

She took a deep breath. Mike was relying on her. He couldn't hear, and she had to be his ears. She could do this. If she didn't, they'd both be in deep shit.

She strained her ears, forcing herself to listen to the men's voices. She couldn't understand much over the rattle of the engine, and her Portuguese was minimal, but she was pretty sure one of the men explained they were looking for escaped prisoners. Shit, it must be a checkpoint, set up to catch her and Mike.

The cab doors opened. They must be searching the driver's area first. Jessica waited a second, weighing their options. Chances were that after the cab, their next stop would be the box where she and Mike hid. If they went now, while the rebels were poking their heads in the truck, they at least had the element of surprise.

She took a deep breath, readied herself, and then before she could overthink it, she leaped up and out of the box. Mike was seconds behind her as she jumped off the bed of the truck and onto the leaf-strewn path. She had a brief glimpse of a surprised face of a man in a haphazard rebel's uniform, before she sprinted towards the trees.

Shouting, gunfire. Jessica ignored them all as she plunged into the undergrowth and kept running. Mike was right behind her. Then, he overtook her, directing her in a jagged path through the jungle so they'd be harder to track. He avoided the thick stands of ferns and vines as best he could, dodging through clearer paths so any pursuers would have a harder time following their trail.

Jessica's breath sawed through her lungs. She could barely breathe, and her head spun, but she didn't dare stop. The shouts of the rebels filtered through the trees behind her, thankfully growing fainter with every step.

She was exhausted. But she had to keep moving.

Dawn had fully risen by the time they finally lost their pursuers. How long had they been in that truck? She didn't know, but she imagined they were now much closer to their destination than they would have been if they'd walked the whole way. Were they close to the border? How much farther until they were safe?

Mike slowed, and after confirming with her that she couldn't hear any signs of pursuit, he stopped. He handed her the canteen, which was running low on water. Two nights had passed since they'd had an opportunity to boil any. Mike had managed to salvage some clean water from condensation on leaves and in tree grooves, but it wasn't enough to sustain them. If they didn't find a stream and build a fire soon, they'd risk dehydration.

They finished off the water, ate some fruit Mike picked, and finished off the nuts he'd roasted so many days ago.

"What's the plan?" she asked.

He sighed. "Honestly, I don't know. I don't know where we are, or how far from the border we are. I can only guess."

He looked more defeated than she'd ever seen him. She frowned, an odd discomfort building in her chest. "Are you okay?" she asked tentatively.

Mike's lips twisted. "I fucked up back there. I never should have let myself get distracted." His jaw clenched.

Jessica's heart sank. The talk she'd so dreaded after the first time they'd kissed hadn't been avoided, only delayed. Dammit. She didn't want to deal with this.

"We both got distracted, but we got out alive. Don't beat yourself up over it."

He narrowed his eyes at her. "It's my duty to protect you. And I put you in danger."

She shrugged. "To be fair, I also put myself in danger, since I initiated it."

"Jessica…"

"What? I did." She narrowed her eyes, daring him to challenge her.

"You shouldn't dismiss this. You were nearly captured today because I let my dick get in the way of my job."

"What would have changed if we'd been paying more attention, hmmm?"

He tilted his head. "What do you mean?"

"I mean, we were traveling along nicely, and then the truck slowed. No reason for us to know anything was wrong at that point. Then, I heard voices, and we knew we were in trouble. At what point would our not having been distracted helped us in that scenario?"

A muscle ticked in his jaw, but he said nothing.

"Exactly," she said with some satisfaction. "So get over yourself. We were having some consensual relaxation time and had a close call. Don't read anything more into it than that."

His eyebrows shot up and the corner of his lip curled. "Relaxation? Is that what the kids are calling it these days?" His eyes heated as his mind clearly cast back to the moment in the box. Jessica's stomach heated in response. She hadn't had an orgasm like that in a long time.

"I don't know about you, but I was pretty relaxed afterward."

He gave a reluctant chuckle, and some of his tension melted away. His hot eyes swept over her and a tingle raced beneath her skin where his gaze touched. "I was anything but relaxed," he murmured in a low voice. He stepped forward. "In fact…" He broke off and made a sound of frustration. "Shit, this isn't the time. But be warned, I will find a way to get inside you, and finish what we started in that damn box."

His gaze was intense. He meant it.

Jessica's stomach clenched. *Yes, please*. She wanted Mike so badly. He was sometimes lacking in manners, but that hardly mattered when it came to sex. The man clearly knew how to please a woman, and that was all that counted.

She smiled, imagining if they were dating, if she invited him to meet her parents. She doubted they'd be impressed with him. Any time they set her up with someone, it was with a man from their own social circles. Urbane. Wealthy. Mike was neither of those things.

The petty, childish part of her enjoyed the thought of bringing someone a bit crude and overtly masculine into their lives. It wouldn't be the first time she'd done something like that to shock her parents. But the idea felt somehow wrong. She didn't want to use Mike like that. She liked him too much, and he deserved better than to be a pawn between her and her parents. If they did continue…whatever this was between them, back in the US, it wouldn't be because her parents wouldn't approve.

It would be because she wanted to.

The idea surprised her. She so rarely regretted only forming temporary attachments to her lovers. But Mike was different. There was something about him that drew Jessica in, made her want to stay with him.

It wasn't only that he was so different to what she was used to, it was that in many ways they were the same. They both traveled the world, helping people. They both believed in being masters of their own destinies. They weren't passive participants in life, they were actively trying to create the world they wanted to see.

What amazing things could they do, if they worked together?

"Once we find me a shower of some kind, I'm up for anything," she told him.

Mike's eyes darkened. "Shit, don't say stuff like that when I can't do anything about it."

She grinned. "Just think about it, big guy. It'll make it all the sweeter when you finally get me naked."

He growled at her, and her grin widened. He was fun to tease. But the truth was, Jessica wanted him as much as he apparently wanted her.

Christ, when the hell would they get home?

CHAPTER ELEVEN

Twenty-four excruciating hours later, Mike stumbled across a small village. It was built in a clearing, with thirty or so houses dotted around the space. The buildings were constructed from wood, but looked sturdy enough.

Locals strode between the buildings, greeting each other, talking, trading wares. The desire to stride into the village without a thought was overwhelming. He couldn't see any sign of rebels, but they were only a day away from the checkpoint where they'd nearly been caught. It wasn't safe to stop.

He glanced at Jessica. She looked worn, exhausted, but she still managed a smile for him. Jesus, he wanted her.

A village meant a bed. Maybe showers. All the things Jessica deserved. Should he take the risk and allow them to stay for the night? Rest up for a long hike tomorrow? He estimated they were still a few days from the border. They'd made up some time in the truck, but not as much as he'd hoped.

He was tempted to risk staying for the night, but he didn't know if that was actually a good idea, or if it was his cock talking. He could justify it all day long, but the reality was that he simply wanted Jessica to be happy. And to have a chance to finally make love to her.

The incident in the box had to rank as one of the hottest of his life, and he hadn't done even a quarter of all the things he wanted to with her.

It had been a week since he'd found her in that camp. Surely one day to rest wouldn't be such a bad idea. Or was he talking himself into it?

"Are we stopping?" she asked after nudging him to grab his attention. A "no" was on the tip of his tongue—they shouldn't risk it—but her bright eyes gave him pause. She was trying so hard not to look excited by the prospect, but there was no way to disguise the energy pouring from her.

Damn it, he should say no.

"Yeah," he said, even while cursing himself. "But we have to stay below the radar."

She did the cutest little jump to express her excitement and then threw her arms around him. Mike held her tight and breathed her in. His heart lifted in joy, and he found he really liked making this woman happy.

She kissed him on the cheek as she drew back and his heart flipped. Damn it, he needed to stop with this emotion shit. There couldn't be anything between them but sex.

His heart didn't listen.

The two of them skirted the edge of the village, getting a lay of the land. They stopped behind a small house with two rooms that looked in worse repair than the rest.

"Stay here," he told Jessica, then crept forward. He peered into the hole that had been cut from the wall that acted as a window. There was no glass, only a tattered curtain covering it. The inside confirmed his suspicions. The place was completely empty. It must have been abandoned.

He glanced around and spotted a tank. Rainwater?

He waved Jessica over. She crept to his side, then peered in the window. "Is this where we're staying?"

"Yes. And I'm hoping it might give us a happy surprise."

Jessica looked intrigued, so Mike grinned and opened the door. It didn't have a lock on it so it swung wide. He stepped inside. It wasn't bad. Hadn't been abandoned too long, or it would have been dirtier and in worse repair.

But Mike didn't stay there long. He strode into the next room and found he was right. A shower. He crossed his fingers and reached for the taps. Lukewarm water sputtered and then sprayed. He laughed, turning in time to see Jessica gasp in delight. Joy lit her face, making her glow.

Whatever happened, that moment had been worth it all. The expression on her face made his heart ache in the best way.

"Don't hate me," he said. "But I'll take the first shower. Then I'll head into the village and see if I can trade for some more interesting food than parrot or fruit."

Jessica pouted, but then nodded. "As long as I get the longer shower," she said.

"Absolutely."

True to his word, Mike was in and out as quickly as possible. He left the soap and Jessica's clothes in there for her and headed back into the main room fully dressed. Jessica had found a fern leaf somewhere and was using it to sweep out some of the dirt.

"Clever," he said, and she grinned.

"My turn?"

"Your turn," he confirmed. She raced past him into the shower and he laughed. As he heard the shower start up again, he dug through his pack for a few items, then headed for the front door.

Normally, he wouldn't have made himself known in a village while laying low, but he figured these people were remote enough that they'd have no way of contacting the rebels. He couldn't see any vehicles around, and the house they'd been in had no electricity. There were no roads to or from the village, only walking trails, so it was clear these people were fairly remote. They wouldn't have a phone. A radio, maybe, but it was a slim chance.

Besides, he and Jessica needed to eat, and something other than fruit. Even if he collected food, they'd need a fire to cook it, and that couldn't go unnoticed. Better to announce themselves now.

He approached an old woman squatting near a fire, poking at leaf-wrapped packages in the coals. She was short and stooped, taking up barely any space. But she had an energy about her. Something in her deeply-lined face that told him this woman shouldn't be dismissed. Wisdom, maybe. Or strength.

She cowered a little when she caught sight of him, and Mike made an effort to appear harmless. He hunched his shoulders and held out his hands in the universal "I don't mean you harm" gesture.

She eyed him warily, but didn't call for help, so Mike took it as a win.

He didn't speak Portuguese. And he couldn't lip read in the language anyway. So he'd have to communicate in the universal language of gestures.

He pointed to the food in the fire. She had a lot, or he wouldn't ask. Then, he pointed to himself. Her expression turned from wary to speculative. She could sense a possible negotiation here, and she was a shrewd woman. He admired that.

She held out her hand, and but Mike didn't have any Zolegan currency. US dollars wouldn't do jackshit in a place this remote.

He swallowed and considered his options. He didn't have anything to trade. Not something he'd want to part with, anyway, considering he and Jessica had another few days in the jungle. It wasn't like he brought non-essentials with him on rescue missions.

Though…he did have one thing that might be valuable to this woman. Something he didn't need to survive.

He pulled Ramirez's coin from his pocket and stared at it. His chest tightened. Jessica's words came to him, the ones about how Ramirez would have given him the coin, even if he'd know the outcome.

And she was right, he would have. Ramirez had cared about his friends more than himself—it was why he'd given Mike the coin in the first place. That was one of the things Mike had always liked best about him. Denying that part of his friend, his protective instincts, hurt him more than the guilt had.

The burden of self-blame that had been dragging at him for so long loosened. He'd always miss his friend, and regret what had happened to him, but he was no longer choked by it. The guilt wasn't gone completely, he didn't think it ever would be. Now, though, it was like he had permission to live in a way he hadn't for a very long time, maybe ever.

This adventure—Jessica—had changed him, and he tasted freedom.

After a moment's hesitation, he held the coin out to the woman. She snatched it, tested it, then gave him a grin and a nod. She stood and disappeared into the house behind her, returning with a precisely-woven basket. She used two sticks to transfer most of the food packets from the fire into the basket, keeping a few for herself.

Mike smiled and nodded at her, and gratefully took the basket. He pointed at one of packets and then at her, offering her to take more, but she shook her head. He hoped she wasn't putting herself out, but she should be able to sell or trade that coin for a lot more than one meal.

He went back to the cabin he and Jessica had chosen. When he reached the door, he turned back to see the old woman eyeing him from her place by the fire. He studied her for a moment, then lifted his hand in a wave. She returned the gesture, then squatted back by the fire to take her own food packets out.

Mike stepped inside the hut, heart thrumming at the thought of seeing Jessica again.

Jessica had never had a better shower. To properly cleanse two weeks of dirt and grime from her skin and hair was one of the greatest pleasures of her life. Right up there with the orgasm Mike had given her last night.

She used some of the remaining water to wash her and Mike's clothes, hoping they'd dry in time for tomorrow. If not, the clothes would soon be damp from their sweat anyway, so it hardly mattered.

While waiting for Mike, she disengaged his sleeping mat from his bag. He hadn't used it yet this trip that she knew of, preferring the hammocks out in the jungle because of the bugs. Now that they were inside, Jessica was hopeful they could sleep closer to the ground.

That way they could share.

She had some plans for that mat tonight, and she hoped more than anything Mike would agree with her.

The door opened, and Mike stepped through. Jessica didn't know which was more mouthwatering. Him, or the food he carried.

"What's that?"

"Mystery food," he said. "But it smells like it has flavor, and probably isn't parrot or fruit, so fingers crossed it's an improvement over our usual fare."

They sat beside each other on the mat and unwrapped the food in the basket. There were two whole fried fish, covered in spices and cooked on a bed of vegetables. There were more vegetables in a different packet. Some kind of meat that Jessica couldn't identify, but wasn't sure she wanted to.

"It's a feast," she said. "But you said we shouldn't eat the fish here."

He shrugged. "If the locals eat it, there's a much higher chance it's safe. I'm willing to be taste tester, if you want."

"No way," she growled. "You'll eat it all before I get a bite."

He grinned unrepentantly and didn't deny it. Jessica's stomach rumbled, and not even the plague could stop her eating the amazing-smelling food.

They dug in. While they did, they talked. More about their lives, their childhoods, what they wanted to do in the future. Jessica neatly sidestepped that last question by telling Mike he needed to thank the chef for the delicious food they were consuming.

"Seriously. I don't know whether this food is simply amazing on its own, or because we've been eating…what we've been eating for the last week. But damn."

Mike nodded his agreement and stuffed another roast vegetable in his mouth.

"It's afternoon now. Are we staying here all night?" she asked, body thrumming with want.

Mike's eyes darkened as his gaze roamed her over. "Yeah," he said hoarsely.

Good. His mind was in exactly the same place as hers. Her belly tightened in anticipation.

They finished the meal and washed up. Mike left to take the basket back to the old lady. Jessica swept the floor again while he was gone. She couldn't help it. She was finally clean—minus clean clothes—and she wanted to stay that way.

But the instant Mike stepped back into the hut, she was distracted from her goal.

He looked so damn good.

Jessica dropped the fern and launched herself at him.

ON THE MOVE

CHAPTER TWELVE

Mike caught Jessica midair, pulling her tightly against him as she wrapped her legs around his waist. Their mouths fused, tongue tangling.

He palmed her butt, kneading it, and Jessica groaned into his mouth. He felt the vibration to his toes. Christ, he was already hard. And hot. So hot.

Her hands fisted in his hair, pulling so tight it was on the edge of painful. It only made him hotter, more desperate for her. He turned them and strode forward until her back hit the interior wall. It moved slightly, but didn't give, so the sensible part of Mike's mind figured it would be safe enough. The rest of him, however, didn't care whether the house crumbled around them, he just needed to be inside Jessica.

Her head tilted back, breaking the kiss as her lungs gasped for air. He watched the movement of her chest expanding, gaze riveting on the way her breasts pushed against his chest. Too tempting. He couldn't resist.

He dipped his head, licking the exposed top of her breast. She tasted clean, with the faint saltiness of sweat. Whatever happened, he would never, ever regret finding her a shower. Not if it led to this.

Her hands ran through his hair in a sensual stroke and her hips rocked, rubbing her clit against his hard cock. He groaned, his fingers digging into her hips. He encouraged the movement, tilting her hips so she'd find her pleasure against him. Mike gritted his teeth at the sensation, keeping himself under control.

Fuck, she felt good.

He returned to her mouth, kissing her like she was air and he needed breath. She wrapped her arms around him and held him tight, still shifting her hips in a sensual dance.

Mike slid his hands from her hips. Up, up, over her ribs until he reached her breasts. He ran his hands over them, memorizing the shape. Jessica arched her back, pressing them more firmly into his palms. Heat spiked at the gesture. The delicious feel of her breasts in his hands was no longer enough. He had to see them.

Breaking the kiss, Mike stared down at Jessica for a long moment, gaze roaming over her face. Her lips tilted up into a smile, and he couldn't help the return gesture. Neither said anything. They didn't need to.

Mike slid Jessica's shirt from her arms and dropped it at their feet. Next, he skimmed his palms up her side, his calloused hands rough against her soft skin. He took her tank top as he went, tugging it over her head and letting it fall. He took his time, enjoying the sight of her in his arms in only a bra.

But Jessica clearly wasn't in the mood to be patient. When he didn't immediately make a move on her bra, she reached up and undid it herself, flinging it across the room.

Her grin turned naughty. "Your turn."

But Mike's eyes were drawn back to her perfect breasts. Full and creamy, with pink nipples standing to attention. If Jessica said anything more, he didn't notice. He plumped her breasts, testing their weight. Then, he dived down and captured a nipple in his mouth. Her moan vibrated through him, strengthening when he rolled the other nipple between his thumb and forefinger.

Her hips began their slow roll again, hardening his cock even further.

Her fingers slid through his hair, pressing him deeper into her breasts. He laved the nipple with his tongue as he tweaked the other. Then, he switched sides, giving her left breast some equal love. When he finally lifted his head, her breasts glistened with his saliva. The sight was unbearably hot, like he'd somehow branded her with a part of himself.

She was the very picture of an aroused woman. Flushed skin, hooded eyes. Possessiveness welled up in him. Something beyond attraction, beyond liking this woman. Something deep and primal.

But now wasn't the time to analyze that. Not when he had a beautiful woman in his arms that he needed to satisfy.

He met her gaze.

"Shirt. Off."

Mike grinned. He liked that Jessica was a woman who knew what she wanted. And he liked even more that she wanted him.

He stripped his shirt over his head to reveal his bare chest. Her gaze riveted there, and Mike had the odd urge to preen. He knew she liked his chest. That had been obvious the first day, when he'd stripped for her. But seeing that lust in her eyes now, in this moment, was something else. Made him proud of his body beyond it being a functional tool, but purely because it pleased her.

Her hands flattened against his chest and she ran her hands over the hard planes of his pecs and abs.

"Your body is insane," she murmured.

"Thank you," Mike said with a grin.

"I want to lick it."

Mike blinked. "Okay."

Jessica unwrapped her legs from around his waist, and Mike had a moment of disappointment he'd agreed. But then she stepped closer—so close her nipples brushed against his chest—and planted a kiss on his right pec.

Mike couldn't take his eyes off her as she kissed and licked her way down his body. Her tongue traced a wet path over his skin, leaving a trail of heat in her wake. He gathered her hair back and fisted it, to make sure he didn't miss a moment. And when she eased onto her knees, all his blood rushed south to pool in his groin.

"Jessica..." he groaned, both a warning and a plea.

Jesus, seeing her in that position, imagining her with her mouth wrapped around his cock, was enough to bring him close to the edge. She reached for the button on his pants and he tensed in anticipation. She glanced up at him from beneath hooded lashes.

"Can I?"

"Please," he gritted out.

She grinned and tugged his pants and underwear down, freeing his cock. Immediately, she wrapped a hand around the base and Mike's hips jerked. His hand tightened in her hair.

"Fuck."

She licked the underside of his cock, and Mike fought to hold still as lightning ran up his spine. Her tongue swirled over the tip. He was torn between closing his eyes to focus on the sensations, and keeping them open so he could sear the hottest sight known to man onto his eyeballs. He chose the latter, knowing he'd want to remember this for the rest of his life.

Jessica sucked him deep into her mouth, and he nearly came right then. He forced himself under control as she worked him with her hand and mouth. He wanted this to last, damn it.

But then Jessica rested her other hand on his thigh. Mike spread his legs, wondering if she was hinting. And when she cupped his balls, he knew he'd been right. There was no way he'd last if she continued this, the fire racing through his veins bringing him ever closer to the edge.

"Enough," he growled.

Jessica stilled, meeting his gaze with her mouth still around his cock. She raised an eyebrow in question.

"I need to be inside you," he explained.

Slowly, with obvious reluctance, she pulled back, still working him with her tongue. Mike took a deep breath and used the moment to restrain himself.

"You've got a great cock," she said, shattering his control all over again. "Almost as nice as your chest."

Mike laughed at her playful expression. She was doing it on purpose to push him, he knew, and he liked that side of her. Liked that she wasn't afraid to tease him, to stand her ground, to get what she wanted.

In fact, he liked her a whole hell of a lot.

"Bed," he bit out.

Jessica stood and backed toward the bed, unbuttoning her pants as she went. Their gazes stayed locked, her eyes challenging.

The second she reached the bedroll, she let her pants and underwear fall to the floor so she was completely naked.

Shit, she was magnificent. Even though she'd lost some weight in the last week—enough that he was determined to feed her well once they got stateside—she was still perfect. A perfect body to go with the perfect woman.

He strode forward, determined to be inside her immediately. But he froze halfway there.

"Shit. Condoms."

He made a detour towards his pack and dug through it, desperately flinging its contents aside until he produced a condom.

He turned to Jessica, holding it up in triumph. Her eyebrows shot up.

"You brought condoms on a rescue mission?" she asked. "And with *whom* were you planning to get lucky?"

He chuckled. "Condoms are useful for many things other than safe sex. Carrying water, and—"

"Okay, okay," she laughed. "Just get over here."

Mike strode forward and snatched her up into his arms. Her legs wrapped around his waist again, positioning his cock right near her entrance. He didn't slide deep, though. Not without the condom.

And not before he tasted her.

He knelt on the bedroll and eased Jessica back until she lay against the fabric. Her legs stayed wrapped around his waist, so he gripped both her ankles and unwound them. She pouted until he shuffled back and spread her legs wide. Then, she got a wicked gleam in her eyes as she realized what he intended.

He focused on her clit first, licking and sucking until her hips moved involuntarily with every stroke of his tongue. Her obvious pleasure shot straight to his groin. She was so free with her passions. It made him exponentially hotter knowing she was honest about how she felt.

He inserted one finger into her, working her until he could comfortably fit two. Right as she was on the edge, her body tense with the need to orgasm, he stopped and pulled back.

Jessica narrowed her eyes at him, a challenge and a warning. He ignored her and searched for the condom, where it must have slipped from his fingers. He found it beneath her left heel and tore open the package. Taking his time, watching her, he rolled it on and then fisted himself.

Jessica's eyes followed the movement with a heated expression.

There were so many things he wanted to do with her. Things he didn't dare think about. This was a one-time thing. A jungle fling. He had to remember that.

He came over her, holding himself on his elbows above her. His cock settled in the cradle of her thighs, but Mike paused for a moment, staring into her eyes. There was something there, something he couldn't quite identify. Something that made his heart thump louder.

Her legs wrapped around his waist, urging him to move. So Mike levered up onto one arm and guided his cock into her.

Her walls clenched around his cock and he tightened his fists as he fought for control.

They both paused at the sensation of him being inside her, adjusting. Reveling. Shit, she felt good. Hot and tight around him. He leaned down to brush his mouth against hers, unable to resist her kiss-plumped lips. As their tongues met, Mike pulled out of her on a slow glide.

Jessica gasped into his mouth. He flexed his hips and slid home. They both groaned in unison, the vibrations mingling between them. They were communicating in that ancient way of the bodies that needed no sound. Like naked sign language.

He moved again, and again, Jessica moving her hips to meet his every thrust. Her hands played over his back, his chest, his ass. As if she wanted to touch every part of him she could reach.

Their sweat-slicked skin glided against each other as he pumped into her. His chest heaved and his muscles clenched with his determination to stay in control.

His orgasm built quickly, the base of his spine tightening in anticipation. He wouldn't come without her. Mike balanced himself on one elbow and reached down. He found her clit with his thumb, brushing over it.

Jessica's back arched. Mike kept thrusting into her, faster now. His thumb didn't stop its dance on her clit, bringing her ever closer to orgasm.

He wished he could hear the sounds she was making. He was sure Jessica's cries of pleasure would be like the sweetest music. But he had to settle for watching her come apart as he hit the exact right spot.

She went rigid, her core clenching around his cock. Her head thrashed from side to side, and still he didn't stop. Then, she came hard.

The sensation of her squeezing his cock sent Mike over the edge. He lost control, slamming into her over and over as he came.

His vision blacked out for a long moment, only returning to find he'd collapsed on top of Jessica.

He rolled off her, checking to make sure he hadn't crushed her. But she gave him a satisfied grin that kicked his heart. Smug male satisfaction welled in him. He'd pleased her. And Jesus, he couldn't wait to do it again.

Unable to help himself, he leaned forward and kissed her. She kissed him back with a dreamy slowness, like their post-sex haze was an airborne drug that made her languid. They parted so that he could simply look at her. She was so damn beautiful.

When sleep pulled at him, he reluctantly got up to dispose of the condom and clean himself up. He pulled on his clothes, even now unwilling to risk mosquito bites or other crawlies. He threw Jessica hers, and she dressed without complaint.

Then, he returned to her bed and spooned around her. He didn't care that it was too hot for that. He couldn't not touch her.

They were drifting to sleep when the door to the house burst open.

CHAPTER THIRTEEN

It wasn't the sound that alerted Mike, it was the way Jessica tensed in his arms. He bolted upright in time to see the door crash open and a group of men stepped through.

Mike dived for his pack and the knife within, only to find his things still strewn across the floor from when he'd hunted for the condom.

Shit, where was his knife? It wouldn't do much against the men with assault rifles, but it would be something. Why the fuck had he let himself get so distracted by Jessica that he'd dropped the ball this badly? He'd put them both in danger for his dick. What a fuck up.

Jessica scrambled into a standing position. Mike gave up on the knife and followed, putting himself between her and the men. The light was low in the room. Only the moonlight through the open doorway and the thin curtain lit the space. It was enough for him to count five men, but not enough to know if they spoke.

He hated being this vulnerable. But he set his jaw in determination. He wouldn't let them get to Jessica, no matter what. Even if he had to die to protect her.

A few flashlights clicked on. Mike winced against the light suddenly shining in his eyes, holding up a hand to cast shade.

A man stepped into view, his face in shadow. He wasn't wearing the tattered, mismatched uniform of the other rebels they'd encountered so far. No, this man was in the full military dress of the Zolgegan army. He had enough medals pinned to his chest to imply an impressive career if they were real, but Mike eyed him warily. Was this guy here to help them? Or hurt them?

He held himself like a true career-military man, his back straight and his eyes shoulder-width apart. Mike's eyes adjusted to the flare of the flashlights, enabling him to see a man in his fifties, with deep bronze skin and close-cropped graying hair. He was sure this was the same guy he'd seen at the airport, the one who had directed the rebels.

"Hello," he said, in heavily accented English, obvious by the way his mouth moved around the words. "I am General Javier Moreno of the Zolegan Rebel Army. You need to come with me."

Mike eyed him. It was definitely the same man from the airport. And, if he wasn't mistaken, this man was the leader of all of the rebels. There was something about the way he stood, and talked, that implied he was the man in charge. Even if he wasn't the true leader, he thought very highly of himself.

"That's not going to happen," Mike told him. "I won't let you use Jessica as a bargaining chip."

Evidence of their lovemaking still clung to the room, to his soul. He couldn't let them take her. Not when she'd cracked open something inside his chest, something that ran deep and pure. He couldn't bear it if anything happened to her. Not before he had a chance to tell her that she'd changed him, and for the better.

"My boy," Moreno said with a paternalistic sneer. "You don't have a choice."

He waved his hand and the other four men stepped forward, guns raised. Mike stilled. It wasn't the worst odds of his career. But since he was unarmed, it was pretty close. Surely they wouldn't shoot and risk hitting Jessica? They needed her alive to extort the money from her parents. As long as she was in the line of fire, they wouldn't fire.

Keeping that in mind, Mike stepped forward to meet the man. Jessica stuck close to his back. Too close, if he'd need to engage in hand-to-hand combat, but she obviously had the same idea as he had about preventing the men from shooting.

Only, when he got closer, two of the rebels dropped their assault rifles and unholstered their handguns from their waists.

Mike's heart thumped. The handguns would be more accurate in close quarters. They might be more willing to take risks.

Mike couldn't stand by and let them try.

He leaped towards one guy, using the element of surprise to disarm him of the handgun. It reminded him that for an army, these guys were poorly trained. He sent his elbow into the man's face, dropping him to the floor, and then quickly turned. He raised the gun to point at the next rebel in line.

But his target was waiting for him, and used the butt of the assault rifle to come down hard on Mike's raised arm. He grunted in pain, his grip on the gun loosening. He forced himself to recover, but his opponent was ready for him, whipping the rifle across his face.

Mike's head twisted painfully with the blow and he stumbled back into Jessica.

Jessica.

"Run," he whispered to her.

He couldn't wait to find out if she obeyed him. He turned back to the rebels and raised the gun he was still holding. He let off a shot, but a rifle butt slammed into his stomach, knocking the wind out of him and sending his shot wide. Mike breathed through the pain and slammed his fist into the man's face. The guy stumbled back, clutching a bloody nose. The other two men strode forward, faces pulled into menacing masks.

Mike held up his fists, ready to fight. But his head swam, making it difficult for his eyes to focus.

That's why, when the butt of the rifle came sailing towards his face, he didn't see it until it was too late.

And his mind went black.

Mike blinked his eyes open and immediately regretted it. His head swirled, making his stomach clench with the need to throw up.

He got a quick glimpse of the room before he had to squeeze his eyes shut again to ward off the nausea. It was small, and built of concrete rather than the wooden structures he'd become accustomed to. They could be closer to the city, then. Either that, or this was a remote place designed specifically as a prison.

He eased his eyes open.

A small, barred window lit the room with pale blue moonlight. The shadow of the bars fell across him, an apt metaphor for his current situation even Mike couldn't fail to notice.

He was on an old mattress. The smell radiating from it was not helping his stomach settle.

Nothing else was in the room from what he could see. There was a solid wooden door in the wall opposite him. It had a large lock, and what looked like a dog-door built into the bottom. No doubt to feed the prisoners food.

As Mike's nausea eased, he slowly sat up. The walls were solid concrete. The window was too small to fit through. If he was going to escape, it would have to be through that door. Was there something he could use to pick the lock?

No. They'd stripped him of everything. He only had the clothes he'd intended to sleep in, so not even boots on his feet. Shit.

He stood and stumbled to the door. Peering through the keyhole didn't get him much more information. Just more gray concrete walls. Was there someone out there? A guard? Impossible to tell without hearing, unless they walked into his line of sight. Mike waited a long moment but had no such luck.

He strode to the window instead, jumping to grasp the bars and haul himself up. They were solidly built, and wouldn't budge without some decent tools.

Outside the window was a small courtyard, surrounded by more buildings similar to the one he was in. There were no people around, but it was clearly late in the evening or into the early hours of the morning.

How long had he been asleep?

And more importantly, what had they done with Jessica in the meantime?

She had to still be alive. She had to.

Jesus, how could he have let this happen? It was his fault. He should have known not to go into the village, or to stay there for so long. He'd only wanted to please Jessica, but instead he'd been stupid. It was his fault she was back in the hands of the enemy. And if anything happened to her—if anything had *already* happened to her—it was all his fault.

He took comfort in the fact that she was no use to them dead.

Which begged the question, why wasn't *he* dead?

Mike understood why they hadn't shot him at the house. Jessica had practically plastered herself to his back, and they wouldn't have wanted to risk hurting her. But once Mike was down, he would've been an easy target. And they could have easily left him there, unconscious or dead, while they made their escape. Instead, they'd brought him with them.

What the hell? What did they want with him?

The door swung open. Mike straightened his spine as General Moreno strode in. He wouldn't let the guy get the best of him this time.

But the general looked in no mood to fight. His expression was pleasant as he smiled at Mike.

Moreno indicated behind him, and a rebel soldier brought in two chairs. He placed them opposite one another, out of arms' reach, and then took a station by the now-closed door. Lights flickered on, bathing the room in an artificial glow.

The general sank into the chair nearest the door and gestured to the one opposite him.

"Please."

Hesitantly, Mike made his way to the chair and sat. He and Moreno stared at each other for a long moment, both waiting for the other to speak. Mike didn't have the patience for politics today. He sat back in the chair and crossed his arms.

"Where's Jessica?"

"She's here. Safe. For now."

"What will you do with her?" Mike asked. He didn't want to have this conversation. He wanted to punch the general in the face and stride out the room to find Jessica. But between the guard at the door—deceptively alert—and an unknown number of people outside the room, Mike knew that wouldn't be the smart play.

It grated him to stay put, but he forced himself to relax and concentrate on what Moreno might say. He didn't want to miss anything, and he was already struggling to lip read the man's English with his heavy accent.

Moreno shrugged. "The same. Record a video with her saying the rescue attempt failed. Demand more money."

"They won't pay," Mike told him.

"To get their only daughter back? I think they will. I think they'll pay any price we ask."

Mike gritted his teeth. The problem was, he wasn't convinced the general was wrong. Despite Jessica's apparently contentious relationship with her parents, they clearly loved her. He'd seen firsthand the worry in their eyes when they'd begged him to find their only child.

"You won't get away with this."

"I think I will."

"She doesn't deserve this, you know. She's a good person." Mike bit off the telling words too late.

The general's eyes sharpened. "Deserve? I'll tell you who doesn't deserve this. My people. They are forced to live under a corrupt rule as this country bleeds them dry for the profit of greedy men. I'm going to change that, no matter what it takes. My people *deserve* better."

"There are other ways of doing that than kidnapping innocent women and extorting money from their parents," Mike told him through clenched teeth.

"We treat her well," Moreno countered. "We haven't hurt her. We didn't even kill you. And as for her parents? The money we ask for is but a drop in a lake for them. They will hardly notice it gone, yet for us it will completely change this country."

"For the better?" Mike asked. "You really think a man who stoops this low will be a good leader for his people?"

Moreno narrowed his eyes. "I will be far better than the rich, greedy fools who call themselves leaders."

"Really? Say this whole plan works. What will you do next time things get difficult for the economy? Find more American heiresses to kidnap for ransom? Face it, you've stooped to their level. You're no better than they are."

Moreno stood, sending the wooden chair back onto the concrete floor. He strode away, his back to Mike. And Mike tensed. Was the man saying something? He didn't know.

Mike's gaze flickered to the guard, and their eyes met, then flicked away. No clues there.

"Well?" Moreno demanded as he turned back around. "How can you accuse me of sinking low, considering the things your own government does to people all over the world?"

The knot in Mike's chest loosened. He didn't have to admit his deafness—a weakness in this situation—or risk looking stupid. "The government of my country is flawed, too, there's no denying that. But it doesn't mean you should do it because everyone else does."

Moreno's expression grew speculative. "You talk as if you have more faith in me and my people than I do. Is that what you truly believe?" He rightened the chair and sat, folding his hands over his stomach. It looked like the general was preparing for a long chat.

Mike still had no idea what was happening here. Why was he debating morality with the man who had kidnapped him and Jessica? Surely Moreno had better things to do than have this conversation?

Or maybe he wanted to be talked out of his actions? Maybe, if Mike chose his words right, Moreno would let him and Jessica go. Was it possible?

He studied the general with new eyes. The man didn't look like he was asking to have his mind changed, but why else would he be here?

"I believe in doing the right thing, the right way, even if it's the harder, slower process," Mike said eventually. "I agree with you that the government of Zolego needs to change. And soon, before it's too late for the people here. But I don't think it's right for you to use people for your own ends. Exploit them, as you are trying to stop your government doing to your own people."

"You have an interesting mind, Michael Ford."

Mike's eyebrows shot up. "So you know my name."

"I know a lot about you. I know about your military career. Your retirement. We've had similar paths, you and I."

"What do you mean?" Mike asked.

"I, too, was discharged from the army after giving it most of my life." He fingered the medals on his chest. "Left out in the cold, as they say. And I found a new cause later in life, as you found your new career."

Mike swallowed. "My new career is nothing like yours. I simply use the skills I learned in the military to continue doing what I do best, helping people."

Moreno raised an eyebrow. "As do I."

Mike swallowed back a retort. He needed to wrest control of this conversation away from Moreno.

"What are you doing here, Moreno?"

The general sat back in his chair. "You mean this old base?" he said, waving a hand. "Nice, isn't it? Used to belong to occupying forces, many decades ago. I've commandeered it for my own use."

Mike shook his head. "No, here. In this room, with me."

Moreno smiled. "Ah. Well, that's simple. I'm trying to figure out whether you're a spy."

Mike blinked. That was not what he'd been expecting.

"A spy?"

"Yes. From my own experience, it's fairly common for Americans to send operatives into unstable countries. My question is: are you here to support my cause, or prop up our farce of a government?"

Mike swallowed. Shit. No wonder Moreno hadn't ordered him killed right away. He wanted to interrogate him, find out what he knew. From Moreno's point of view, Mike must look suspicious. A highly-trained, former military operative, sneaking into the country and messing with a rebel mission. Yeah, Mike would be suspicious, too.

Moreno probably believed he was here to either destabilize the country further, or gather intelligence on the rebel operations for the Zolegan government at the behest of the Americans.

This wasn't good.

"I can assure you, I'm simply on a rescue mission. I was hired to find Jessica and bring her home."

"Hired by who?"

"Her parents."

"And how did they find you?"

"I work for a company called Soldering On Security. We work out of Portsboro. You can check our website, and there are plenty of local news stories about us. We've recently expanded into international territories when required."

Moreno was silent, eyeing Mike for a long moment. Mike held still, betraying no hint of nerves.

"It's a good story," Moreno said eventually. "And even if it's true, there's no reason to think Senator Vanderslice didn't give you a secondary mission while you are here."

Of course he'd think that. Mike blew out a breath. His position was precarious here. He should've considered how his mission would look from the outside. But he never thought he'd be caught. If all had gone to plan, he would have been out of the country the same afternoon he'd rescued Jessica.

"I can see why you might think that," Mike said carefully. "But I assure you that Senator Vanderslice was only focused on having her daughter returned safely."

Moreno tilted his head, studying Mike. Foreboding crept down Mike's spine. What was this man planning? Whatever it was, Mike was sure it wouldn't be good.

"I thought you might deny it. Normally, I would consider torturing you for the truth. But we both know that rarely works to extract the correct information, hmmm? And I'm not an animal who would hurt another for no purpose."

That point was debatable, but Mike was too relieved from the apparent lack of torture in his future that he didn't call Moreno on it.

"However, you do have a clear weakness. The Vanderslice girl."

The bottom dropped out of Mike's stomach as he stared at Moreno.

"I think, if we torture *her*, you'd be far more forthcoming."

Mike's chest squeezed. "Don't do that. I've told you the truth." He knew his voice was coming out panicked, but he could stop it. Not Jessica. He could withstand the torture, but he couldn't bear for Jessica to get hurt at his expense.

"I'm not a complete monster," Moreno said, as if he hadn't heard Mike. "I won't make you watch. I think her screams would suffice, no?"

"You won't hurt her. You need her alive for the ransom."

"Alive, yes. Whole? I believe that would be negotiable."

Mike swallowed past a thickening throat and shook his head. "Please don't."

"Bring her into the next room," Moreno said to the guard. "I want him to hear her screams."

Moreno stood, turning his back on Mike to leave the room.

The intense, miserable irony of the situation penetrated Mike's haze of panic. To his own surprise, he laughed.

Moreno whipped around. "You laugh. You want your woman to be hurt?"

Mike swallowed the bitter laughter. "Of course not. But if you want to use her against me like this, hearing her screams won't be enough."

Moreno turned all the way around, a confused frown on his face. "You are so callous you wish to see your woman be tortured?"

"Of course I don't want to see that. But if you want me to react to the torture, we'll have to be in the same room. I'm deaf, Moreno." At least he'd get to see her if they brought her here. And being together would give him and Jessica a greater chance of escaping.

Moreno stared at him. "That, in your file, was true? But we've been talking just now."

"I'm reading your lips. It's a bit harder with you because you have a heavy accent, but I can understand enough."

"That's…" Moreno stopped. He looked completely taken aback, and Mike had a moment of satisfaction that he'd managed to put the man on the back foot. And then knowledge slammed into Mike.

Moreno hadn't really meant to torture Jessica. He clearly had some kind of charade or set up to make Mike *think* she was being hurt.

The general wasn't as bad as Mike had feared. Yeah, he'd still kidnapped Jessica—twice—but at least he wasn't a gung-ho torturer. Small mercies.

"Fine," Moreno snapped eventually. "Have it your way. We'll bring the woman to you."

With that, Moreno strode out. And Mike's stomach dropped.

What the fuck had he done?

CHAPTER FOURTEEN

Jessica paced the small room.

Where had they taken Mike? She hadn't seen him since they'd knocked him out. After that, they'd thrown a bag over her head and dragged her through the jungle for a while before throwing her into a car. She hadn't seen any of the journey. They'd tied her hands so she couldn't remove the bag, and only untied her once she'd been marched into this cell.

She didn't even know if they'd brought Mike with them. For all she knew, he could still be lying unconscious back at the village.

Or dead.

Her heart clenched and tears threatened. She breathed deep and clenched her shaking fists to stay in control. She wouldn't accept that. Wherever he was, he was alive.

He had to be. She cared about him too much. She swallowed painfully as that revelation hit her. It hadn't only been physical attraction between her and Mike. She liked him. A lot. She liked his calm under pressure, his ability to rethink plans at the last second. His respect for her, and the protectiveness he showed.

And the amazing sex hadn't hurt. He'd read her body like a book and it had been the hottest thing she'd ever experienced.

But this ache in her chest wasn't an intense afterglow from amazing sex. She cared about him. More than she had about any other guy she'd dated.

And here they were, separated. With her trapped in the compound of a rebel leader who wanted to ransom her to fund his regime. She'd been sympathetic to their cause—still was. But Mike was right. They were going about change the wrong way. She couldn't accept any group that kidnapped an innocent woman—twice—and hurt the man who'd only wanted to protect her.

If they'd killed Mike…

Well, she'd never let them get away with it. She'd use any and every power at her disposal to make them pay.

The door swung open. Jessica whirled around to see a woman standing in the doorway. She was demurely dressed, in a buttoned shirt and skirt that hung to her ankles. A dark braid hung over one shoulder. Her eyes were lowered to the ground in an apparent display of meekness. A servant, or even a slave? Jessica suspected the rebels would have staff to help run things—cooks and cleaners and such—but she didn't want to make assumptions. The woman may only be acting subservient to catch Jessica off guard.

But for what?

It was then that Jessica noticed the rope dangling from the woman's hands. She folded her arms across her chest.

"You don't need to tie me up. I won't escape."

The woman raised her gaze and stared at Jessica blankly.

Jessica tried again, this time in bad Portuguese. "Por favor não me ligue."

The woman shook her head and let out a string of Portuguese too fast for Jessica to follow. She gestured with the rope, and Jessica took that to mean she wouldn't let Jessica go untied. Still, at least the woman hadn't mentioned the bag over her head.

Jessica hoped this meant that she would be taken somewhere other than this cramped room. If she got a better view of the place, she might be able to figure out the best way to escape. And she would escape. No way would she let General Moreno extort her parents. They didn't deserve that, if they'd even pay—which Jessica still wasn't certain of. It would also set a bad precedent, and General Moreno would think he could get away with these kinds of tactics next time. And if her parents didn't pay? Well, chances were Jessica would be screwed.

Jessica eyed the woman in front of her. Should she make a move now, while she had the element of surprise? This woman would be easier to defeat than the general, or any of his men.

But then a guard stepped up behind the woman, glaring at Jessica. He cradled his assault rifle as if he itched to use it. Jessica swallowed and stepped forward with her hands out, capitulating to the woman's request. Better that she get a good assessment of her situation before making any plans. She figured that was what Mike would say, anyway. He liked to recon first, before he made a call.

Thinking of Mike again was like a punch to the stomach, and Jessica let out a shaky breath. She hoped more than anything that he was okay.

The woman cinched the rope around Jessica's wristed and tied them tight. Then, she indicated with her head for Jessica to follow her into the hallway outside the room. Jessica did, noting everything she could see.

Besides the guard she'd seen earlier, who now followed her down the hall, there were two other men guarding the door. The corridor was otherwise empty of people, but there were doors leading off that could house any number of people.

They turned right at a t-junction. The corridor they'd been on continued down to a set of double doors. Jessica ran her gaze over it as they turned. Was it an exit? She didn't have a definitive answer before they were out of sight.

Two doors down, they stopped. A guard was posted on either side of it. Jessica nearly ran into the woman leading them, so distracted was she by her assessment of the guards. The man behind her also stopped in Jessica's personal space, but she had no doubt that was intentional. His hot breath on her neck made her shudder in distaste.

The woman knocked and the door swung open from the inside. She stepped away and indicated Jessica precede her into the room. Jessica hesitated a moment, not sure what she'd find in the room beyond. But then a sharp poke in the back had her stumbling forward. She turned to glare at the guard who'd nudged her with his gun. He gave her a smug grin in return.

Jessica rolled her eyes and stepped into the room without another glance back. The first thing she saw was Mike, tied to a chair with his arms behind him. He appeared unharmed, and her heart soared. He was okay. Better than okay. The way his arms were tied behind his back made his bicep muscles bulge and his shirt pull across his chest. Given their situation, she really shouldn't be noticing things like that. But he was so built it was difficult *not* to notice.

Their gazes met, and his expression tightened. Regret and apology mingled in his gaze, so strong Jessica nearly stumbled back. Her stomach tightened. What had he done to look at her like that?

A movement to her left caught her eye and General Moreno stepped into view. He looked the same as he had in the village house. Tall, straight-backed, radiating command.

"General," she said as a greeting. Her mother had always taught her to be polite when dealing with your adversaries. A woman would be deemed over-emotional if she was passionate about anything, such as swearing a blue streak at the asshole who kidnapped you.

"Miss Vanderslice. Glad you could join us."

Like she had much choice. Instead of saying that, however, she smiled and inclined her head. There was no reply that was both the truth and polite, so she chose to say nothing.

"Your friend and I have reached a bit of an impasse here, and I'm hoping you can help."

Jessica's gaze flickered to Mike in confusion, but he was too busy glaring at Moreno in frustration and anger to give her any hint about what might come next.

"What did you have in mind?" she asked.

"I want you to persuade your friend to tell me the truth."

Jessica frowned. "What truth?" Was Mike hiding something? If he was, it was from her, as well.

"The truth about his mission here. About how he was sent to gather intelligence and destabilize my hold on power."

Jessica's eyebrows shot up. What the hell? She glanced at Mike. This time he looked right at her.

"It's not true." His voice was steady and sure. She wanted to believe him. Surely that was the truth. Because in the week she'd known him, he'd made no effort to gather any information on the rebel camps. In fact, he'd stayed as far away from any hints of the rebels as possible. He wasn't willing to risk his true mission—keeping her safe—for any information.

So why did the general think he would?

"I have no idea what you're referring to." If he believed she was a weak link who would blurt out Mike's plans—plans she didn't even know, and likely didn't exist—then he was sadly mistaken.

"Yes, I didn't think you would. You were the excuse to enter the country, not a partner. I do wonder if they placed you here as bait for my plans, but that might be a little too clever, even for a United States Senator."

Jessica nearly choked. He thought her mother was behind this? It was true Senator Vanderslice could be ruthless and manipulative, but she generally kept that to her home city of Portsboro. It would be highly unusual for her to meddle in international affairs. Even if the president suggested she use her daughter's kidnapping as an excuse, Jessica didn't think she would. Right?

Or maybe she would. Maybe there was something in this for her Jessica hadn't considered. Her mother often played a long game Jessica couldn't even begin to fathom.

She chanced another glance at Mike. That apology was still in his eyes. Why was he sorry? Did that expression mean everything the general said was true? Mike had used her? She didn't want to believe it. Not after what she and Mike had been through together. But she wouldn't put it past her mother to manipulate a man for her own ends. And Mike would have no other reason to feel bad about the general's accusations, so what else could it mean?

Betrayal rose up, choking her. Her mother? Mike? Had they conspired without her?

Now wasn't the time to think about it, even if it overwhelmed her thoughts. Her hurt now was nothing to what might happen to her at General Moreno's hands. She still didn't know what he wanted from her, and that made her nerves ratchet to breaking point.

"If you don't think I know anything, why am I here?" she bit out. She needed time to think, to sort through these new accusations and possibilities. She wanted to trust Mike, but her mother was a different matter. She'd been burned by that woman more than once.

But with Moreno in the room, Jessica didn't dare let her concentration slip.

"I know perfectly well your lover here would never break under torture. It's a sure way to get bad information, anyway."

At the word "torture", Jessica's stomach sank to her toes. Her lungs squeezed. Surely he didn't mean…

"However, he obviously has a fondness for you. And I'm willing to see if he breaks when it is *you* being hurt."

Jessica rocked back on her heels as if she'd been struck. All the blood drained out of her head and the room spun. He planned to torture her? So blatantly?

Was that what the apology in Mike's eyes had been about? Surely not. This wasn't his doing.

"Don't do this, Moreno." It was Mike, pulling at the ropes binding him to the chair. "I already told you I'm only here to rescue her. Your fantasy about me being a spy is just that: your imagination."

"We'll see," Moreno said. He glanced over Jessica's shoulder. "Tie her down."

"Wait," she said, voice ringing through the room. Even Moreno stopped at her command. "Don't you need to give some kind of proof of life to my parents? Record a video like you did last time?"

Moreno eyed her speculatively. "As you said, we already have one."

"Yes, but my parents must know Mike rescued me. You'll need to convince them you have me all over again."

Moreno pursed his lips. "I suppose. But we can always do that later."

"You think they'll pay if I'm beaten and bloody? No way. And what if I can't handle the torture?" she asked, stumbling over the last word. She couldn't let herself picture the reality of what that word meant for her. "What if I die, before you record the video? Then you really won't get your money."

A muscle in Moreno's jaw ticked. She held his gaze, not backing down. This was a stay of execution, nothing more. But if she could delay as long as possible it would give her—and Mike—more chance to escape.

"Fine," he spat eventually. "It's getting late, anyway. We'll record the video tomorrow morning, and begin our…interrogation in the afternoon." He paused. "I suppose it wouldn't hurt to wait. Make you imagine all the things we might do to you. All the hurt we'll cause."

Jessica tried not to look too pleased that the general wasn't planning to torture her right away. Moreno strode behind her to whisper something to the guard inside the door.

While they conversed, she chanced a glance at Mike. Pride shone in his eyes. She sent him a small smile. Even if he had done all the things Moreno had accused him of, for now, they were in this mess together. If he had betrayed her, she could allow herself to feel the sting of that only when they were safe.

They had to escape. And soon.

While Jessica had his attention, she waved her bound hands slightly so his gaze would drop lower. As soon as his eyes were on his hands, she indicated a square as best she could and gave him the sign for one. Then, she put her thumb and forefinger an inch apart, and drew them out to signify the corridor, and then the symbol for two. Finally, she turned her hands and made the corridor sign again, this time at a different angle. She pointed at herself, and indicated the two guards stationed there. She pointed right, and he glanced up at her face in confusion at the last part.

"Maybe exit," she mouthed. At least, she hoped that's what it was. His expression cleared, and he grinned at her.

Moreno whirled around and paced behind Mike's chair. "Take her back to her cell to wait."

One of the guards roughly grabbed Jessica's arm and dragged her out of the room. Her last sight was of Mike's face, eyes riveted on hers like he was memorizing her.

Their plan—such as it was—had to work. It had to.

CHAPTER FIFTEEN

Mike liked having back up plans and options. He liked to recon areas before he went charging in. Going in blind—and, in his case, deaf—was a sure way to get himself and other people killed.

But right now he didn't have many options. He sure as shit wouldn't let Jessica get tortured, so he had to get her out of here tonight. Luckily, he was a master of thinking on his feet.

It was still dark outside the window, and Mike had no idea how much time had passed. It must after midnight, maybe even close to dawn. He hadn't seen anyone move past the window, telling him the compound was well and truly settled for the night.

First, he needed to get out of this room. Then, he'd find Jessica, and get them both the hell out of this place. Beyond that, he had no plan.

But the other options were far worse.

Mike paced the room. There wasn't a lot of space, but he needed to think. The walls were solid concrete, so not much chance of getting through those. He'd already concluded that the window was too small, so that left the door.

It was too solid to break through. He tried the hinges, but they were stuck fast. Without a tool, he didn't have much hope of dismantling them and opening the door that way. Moreno hadn't even left the chair in the room, for him to break apart and use as a weapon. He glanced up at the light fitting, currently bathing him in the harsh artificial glare of fluorescent bulbs. Maybe there was something he could do with that?

Movement in the corner of his eye stopped his thoughts. He spun in time to see a hand opening a little hatch at the bottom. The hand disappeared, and then returned, pushing a tray of food in Mike's direction.

Mike didn't glance at the food, didn't think. He dived forward, landing heavily on the concrete floor. He caught the wrist before the hatch closed, holding on with all his might.

The arm tugged, but Mike didn't let go, arm muscles straining to keep his grip. A face appeared in the hatch, wide-eyed with panic. Mike didn't let himself have a moment of sympathy or hesitation. He gave the man the slightest bit of slack—enough for him to pull away from the door—and then he tightened his grip and yanked.

The door shuddered as the man's head plowed into it. The arm in Mike's grip slackened and the man's unconscious body fell into view.

Mike grinned to himself, but didn't allow himself to stop and celebrate. Someone could be along any minute and raise the alarm. Hell, there might already be someone out there yelling, and he'd never know.

He used both hands to maneuver the unconscious body until he could reach the man's pocket. He dug inside one, and then the other, finally producing a key that might open his door.

He stood and unlocked it, peering out. A scared face came into his field of vision. It was a young man, barely older than a teen, sweaty with terror, hands unsteady where he held the assault rifle in Mike's direction.

Mike didn't pause. He stepped forward and disarmed the kid before he hurt someone—himself included. The kid was too afraid to even get one shot off, for which Mike was grateful.

He gave the young man an apologetic smile and then whacked him over the head with the butt of the rifle, sending him sprawling next to his friend.

Mike glanced up and down the corridor, but he couldn't see anyone else. He shouldered the gun and headed right, in the direction Jessica had indicated. His feet were bare against the cold concrete. Shit, he hoped he'd interpreted Jessica's signs correctly. She was clever, his Jessica. She'd known he'd want recon, and she'd given him what she could.

Pride and affection welled up within him. It was too soon for him to call this feeling love, but it was so close as to be barely indistinguishable from the whole thing. And Christ wasn't that a fuck up. The white trash ex-military man head over heels for a senator's daughter and the wealthiest heiress in the country.

He had to find her, make her understand all the shit Moreno said wasn't true. He'd seen the spark of betrayal in her eyes and it cut him deep that she'd believe it of him. But Moreno was so sure his little fantasy was true he no doubt sounded very convincing. Mike couldn't let Jessica keep thinking that.

Not if he wanted her in his life.

And he did, damn it all to hell. He shouldn't, but he couldn't help himself. He had no idea if she'd have him, but once they were home and safe, he'd have to ask. Because he had no intention of letting her go.

He moved forward until he reached the t-junction. He glanced left, first. As Jessica had indicated, two guards stood outside a closed door. Jessica's cell?

Mike ducked back into the corridor, but the guards hadn't seen him. They were too busy staring blankly at the wall. Mike shook his head. Untrained, the lot of them.

He stuck his head out again, looking right this time, noting double doors at the end of the corridor. The possible exit Jessica had mentioned. Mike eyed it. How sure was she that was the way out?

He turned back to the guards, and they were still stupidly bored. The gun sat heavy in his hands. Should he use it, and risk drawing the attention of everyone in the compound? Jessica would say no. Or she would have, a week ago. He had no idea how she felt about these rebels now that she'd been kidnapped a second time and threatened with torture. Probably not very fondly.

Mike considered his options, then stuck his head around the corridor again.

This time, he whistled low, drawing the attention of the two guards, but hopefully not loud enough for anyone else to hear. One caught sight of him, and Mike ducked his head back around the corridor.

He counted, estimating the steps required to reach him, and then swung out the gun. It struck one guard perfectly between the eyes as he rounded a corner. He slumped the ground. The other guy stared stupidly at Mike for a long moment, giving Mike time to whack the guy between the eyes with the butt of the rifle.

Mike made a sound of disgust as the man fell. This was too easy. If he had a rebel army, there's no way he'd let them wander around so untrained. It was embarrassing.

But he wasn't planning on looking a gift horse in the mouth, so he crouched and extracted a key ring from the guard's pocket. There were an assortment of keys on there. A few that were clearly for cars as well as the ones for the cells.

Mike glanced down the corridor. Empty. He padded lightly along until he reached the door the guards had stood in front of. He inserted a few keys into the lock until he found the right one and swung the door open.

Light from the corridor poured into the dark room. A figure on the bed sat up, then scrambled to their feet. Before he knew what was happening, Jessica had launched herself at him and he snatched her out of the air, her legs wrapping around his waist. It was fast becoming his favorite position.

And that made him think of their night together and he hardened immediately. He dropped the gun he'd been holding and cupped her face, kissing her fiercely. All this talk of torture had wrecked him. He hadn't wanted to imagine her that way—broken and bleeding. And now she was in his arms, healthy and whole. He couldn't resist kissing her, showing his mind and body that she was alive.

Jessica didn't mind. She kissed him back passionately, gripping his hair as her legs tightened around him.

He could stay like that forever, with her in his arms. A small, rational part of his brain sent a warning clang through his mind. His eyes startled open and he remembered where they were. This had to wait until they were safely out of here.

He reluctantly pulled his mouth from Jessica's and looked into her eyes. "You okay?" he asked.

"Yes. We should get out of here." With her sultry, just-kissed gaze, the words were more like a sexy invitation than a plea to get the two of them to safety. His cock reacted, even as his mind focused on the mission once again.

"Let's go."

She jumped down and Mike picked up the gun he'd dropped. The corridor was still empty, other than the unconscious bodies, and thank God for that. He didn't want to get caught because of his dick *again*.

He took Jessica's hand. "The double doors were the exit you meant?"

"I think so. Could be totally wrong. I didn't have a chance to test them."

He shrugged. "It's as a good a chance as any."

They jogged towards the door. Mike glanced at Jessica, and she put her ear to the door, as if she already knew what he'd ask.

"Empty," she mouthed.

He pushed the door open. It didn't lead to the outside, only to another corridor. Mike sighed. Maybe they should go back the other way? He glanced behind them, only to catch sight of guards rounding the corridor on the other end.

"Shit," he muttered, then backed through the door, pushing Jessica behind him. The guards at the other end caught sight of them and raised their guns. Mike didn't think they'd fire—surely Jessica was still too precious to them—but then the muzzles flashed and bullets embedded in the walls next to them.

Mike stumbled back and the door swung shut. "Fuck," he muttered. He'd been hoping their good luck would keep running until they got off the compound. But either the guards were acting independently of Moreno, or he'd finally decided Mike and Jessica were more trouble than they were worth.

They turned and ran. He hoped like hell this corridor went somewhere. He could only see an empty wall at the end.

Jessica turned back, and Mike assumed their pursuers had crashed through the door. His heart pounded as he pushed Jessica ahead of him. He couldn't let a bullet catch her. Concrete sprayed across his face as a bullet hit the wall closest to him. Another corridor broke off from the one they were on and Mike didn't think. He grabbed Jessica's hand and dragged her down it.

Another set of double doors lay at the end. His heart dropped, but they couldn't stop or change direction. He had to keep moving.

They reached the doors before the guards fired and Mike crashed through them, stumbling into the fresh air.

He braked, taking a second to get his bearings. Wire fencing ran on either side. In the distance, a cracked, paved road stretched along the edge of the jungle beyond. They clearly weren't as remote as the first compound had been. Could they be near a city?

He had no idea. And he didn't have time to stop and find out.

A group of Jeeps were parked outside of the building. Perfect. Mike headed towards one and went around the far side. He was conscious of the guards on their tail. He wouldn't have long.

He vaulted into the driver's seat. "Get in the back and stay down," he said to Jessica. He waited long enough to see her do as he said and then he focused on the controls in front of him. Keys. He needed keys.

He dug the key ring he'd pilfered from the guard out of his pocket. *Please be the correct keys.*

The door they'd come through burst open again, four men spilling out into the night. Mike jammed a key into the lock and turned. To his surprise, the engine roared to life, rumbling beneath him. He didn't question it. Throwing the car into reverse, he backed out of the space as the men raised their guns into formation. Mike didn't hesitate. He slammed the gear shift and flattened his foot on the accelerator.

The Jeep leaped forward and barreled towards the men. Two brave men pulled the trigger anyway, not taking the time to get out the way of the speeding vehicle. Mike ducked as the bullets came flying towards them. The windshield shattered, spraying glass all over him. Mike ignored the sting of the small pellets of safety glass. Instead, he peered over the dash to see the two remaining soldiers had finally scrambled out of the way.

Mike swerved towards the road. In the rearview mirror, General Moreno threw open the doors and strode out. He yelled orders, and men scrambled to obey. They'd probably chase them in the remaining cars. Mike wished he'd had the time to disable them, but he'd have to lose them on the road, instead. If at all possible.

"You okay?" he shouted back to Jessica as he turned onto the road. A thumbs up came into his field of vision and he grinned. She stayed in the back seat, away from the shattered glass, but she was okay.

"Stay down," he said, eyeing the rearview mirror. "They'll be on our tail any minute."

How could he lose them? The road was straight, and he couldn't see any offshoots. The road behind him didn't look any better.

He pulled the gun from his shoulders and passed it back to Jessica. "If they get too close, aim the gun in their direction and lay down cover fire. Should get them to back off."

She took the gun from his hands and Mike assumed that meant she'd heard the instructions.

Okay, a plan. He always had a plan.

A bullet embedded into the windshield frame and Mike sank lower in the seat, heart in his throat. If they fired so indiscriminately, they clearly no longer cared if Jessica lived or died, and that made his life a hell of a lot harder.

He glanced around the Jeep, seeing if there was anything he could use. Was that a satellite GPS unit?

He bounced his gaze between the road and the machine as he powered it up. It loaded for a long moment, and impatience made his pulse race. Finally, a red dot on a map flashed. Their location? He squinted to read the coordinates in the dark.

Wait, that couldn't be right. If that was their location, then the border into Colombia would be right...

There.

Ahead of them, a tollbooth loomed out of the dark. Uniformed soldiers stood to attention outside. Mike pressed the accelerator as hard as it would go and the Jeep lurched forward. If they could only get across, they'd be safe.

But then the soldiers ahead of him raised their weapons. No wonder. Someone barreling down on a foreign border like this would make any guards nervous. They were so close.

So Mike did the only thing he could think of.

"Get ready to run," he yelled back to Jessica.

Then, he spun the wheel so the Jeep went perpendicular to the road and skidded to a stop. He launched out of the car at the same time as Jessica. They both landed hard and rolled in the dirt. But Mike didn't stop to catch the breath that had been knocked out of him. He hauled Jessica up and they ran towards the checkpoint with their arms up. Thankfully, Jessica had left the gun behind.

The soldiers looked ready to shoot them on sight. But then the Zolegan rebels fired, and the soldiers turned their attention to the more immediate threat. It gave Mike a chance to shove Jessica through the checkpoint, past the startled guards.

Once they were a safe distance away from the action and hidden by the tollbooth, Mike knelt to the ground and pulled Jessica with him. They both put their hands behind their heads to show they weren't a threat. The Colombian guards approached them cautiously, guns drawn.

"Asylum," Mike said clearly. "We seek asylum."

CHAPTER SIXTEEN

Mike tugged at the tie around his throat. He hated the things. But considering he was about to enter the home of a US Senator and one of the richest men in the country—not to mention the woman he'd fallen for—Mike figured it was worth the sacrifice.

He swallowed as he pushed the doorbell. He hadn't seen Jessica for five days. Not since the political complications of their race across the border had been smoothed out by Senator Vanderslice's people, and Charlie had flown them back to the states.

Would Jessica even want to see him? He had to assume he was here with her permission, but was it for the reasons he hoped? Because he didn't plan to leave this place without her.

Did she believe he hadn't had an ulterior motive in rescuing her? And how did she feel about him?

They'd been through a lot together in the rainforest. Maybe she wanted to forget the whole thing.

Forget him.

The door swung open, and Mike pasted a smile on his face. A man he didn't recognize opened the door, and the white gloves immediately gave him away as a butler. Rich people still had those? He'd thought that was just in movies. For once, one of his weird views about rich people had turned out to be less strange than the reality.

"Hey, man," he said. "The name's Mike Ford. I was invited to dinner tonight."

"Please come in Mr. Ford."

Mr. Ford. Jesus.

"Call me Mike. Not even my dad was Mr. Ford."

The butler's mouth twitched but he said nothing. Mike stepped inside and stopped short. He was in a large foyer. Lush cream carpet swallowed the shiny shoes he'd borrowed for the occasion. The walls were the color of biscuits and decorated with tasteful watercolors. The furniture, what little of it in the room, was tasteful and well-constructed. A carpeted staircase was against the far wall, leading to the upper floors of the house.

Mike had expected marble and gilt. Instead, the house was reasonably comfortable, if huge and spotlessly clean. Maybe this wouldn't be torture after all.

He turned to the butler, and the man's face was scrupulously pleasant. "This way, please."

Mike turned to follow him, but a movement at the top of the stairs caught his eye, and he froze.

Jessica stood there, in a knee-length red dress that hugged her like a second skin. The neckline dipped low, revealing the top of her breasts, and her arms were bare. Her shiny hair was swept up into a complicated-looking knot, revealing the long line of her throat.

His breath caught in his chest. She was the most beautiful woman he'd ever seen.

A slow smile curved across her face. Mike couldn't take his eyes off her as she came down the steps. It wasn't until she was right in front of him that she said anything.

"Hi."

He grinned. "Hi." His gaze swept over her and she did a twirl for him.

"Better than the ratty cargo pants and shirt I wore, huh? I burnt those the second I could."

Mike's heart flipped. "I didn't mind the cargo pants." In fact, he'd liked her that way. Adventurous, strong, approachable.

Now, she looked like the untouchable socialite he'd always know she was. His gut clenched. This would be a lot harder than he'd imagined.

"How have you been?" she asked.

Thinking about you every minute. He cleared his throat. "Fine. I've been forced into a lot of debriefings with Duncan and Mandy, but that's all right. You?"

"Taking lots of showers," she said on a laugh. "And obviously my parents needed to know every detail of what happened."

"*Every* detail?"

She blushed. "Well, I kept some things to myself."

Thank God for that. "And are things okay? With your parents, I mean."

"Yeah," she said, and she seemed genuinely happy. "They're better than they have been in a long time, actually. We're finally having some honest conversations. Thank you for that."

"What did I do?"

"You made me see they really cared, and gave me the confidence to confront them instead of running away. It's changed things for us."

"I'm really glad."

Christ, he wanted to hold her. Where the hell did they stand?

He stepped forward and took her hand. Their fingers tangled together. Belatedly, he glanced around for the butler, but the man had disappeared.

His gaze met hers. Was that hope in her gaze? "Jessica—"

Over Jessica's shoulder, Senator Vanderslice and her husband walked into the room. Mike stepped away from Jessica immediately, snatching his hand away. His palms grew damp. He and Jessica weren't even together—officially, yet—but he was still meeting her parents. Even though this was the second time he'd encountered them, it was worse than the first, because it was far more momentous.

He wasn't meeting clients, he was meeting the people he hoped might one day become his in-laws.

"Senator Vanderslice. Mr. Vanderslice. Nice to see you both again."

Jessica's father stepped forward and held out his hand. "Thank you for saving our daughter. We'll owe you more than you can ever know."

Mike glanced at Jessica, who beamed at him, so he shook the man's hand. "It was my pleasure," he said, and then instantly regretted the word. He should *not* be thinking about pleasure while Jessica stood next to him in that dress.

"And thank you for agreeing to this dinner," Senator Vanderslice said. "It's hardly enough to thank you."

He didn't tell them that he'd only accepted because it gave him an excuse to see Jessica. He hated unnecessary praise, and rescuing Jessica had only been him doing his job. He deserved no additional thanks for that.

But now he had a chance to figure out where he and Jessica stood. And if her parents were more inclined to like him purely because he'd done his job, he wouldn't ruin that.

He glanced at the woman he'd spent one of the most interesting, life-changing weeks of his life with. He needed to get her alone, so they could talk. Would he have to wait until after dinner? That would be an excruciating meal, sitting there making small talk with her parents when he had no idea how she felt about him.

Having a plan for every occasion was his specialty. He was about to make some excuse to get Jessica out of the room, when Jessica spoke first.

"Mom, Dad. How about you go check on dinner? I need to talk to Mike."

Far less subtle than he'd planned, but he'd take it.

Her parents shared a smile, and then nodded. Soon, he was alone with Jessica in an opulent lobby, feeling very out of place, and he suddenly had no idea what to say.

Jessica, apparently, had no such problems. She gripped his face in both of her hands and pulled him down for a kiss. He didn't waste time, gripping her hips over the silky fabric of the dress and pulling her closer. He tilted his head for a better angle, deepening the kiss.

Her parents were in the next room, and the butler could pop up at any minute, but Mike didn't care. Jessica was in his arms and everything was right in the world.

They broke apart, panting, and Jessica grinned at him. "I've wanted to do that for days. I missed you."

"Me, too. I wasn't sure what would happen tonight, where we stood." He paused and took a deep breath. Time to take the plunge. "I want to be with you, Jessica. I fell in love with you somewhere in that jungle, and I don't ever want to let you go."

Tears sprang to Jessica's eyes even as she smiled. "Oh, Mike. I want to be with you, too."

"So you didn't believe all that stuff about your mother hiring me to spy on the rebels?"

She scoffed. "No. Nothing in your actions told me General Moreno's theory was correct."

"Good," he said with satisfaction. She'd believed in him, trusted him.

He kissed her again, unable to help himself. Her mouth was so sweet. He could spend a lifetime kissing her and never get tired of it.

They came apart again, and Jessica grinned. "I have a surprise for you."

Mike eyed her dress. "Is it what's under here? Because I can't wait to find out."

Jessica laughed. "You've already seen all that, so it doesn't count as a surprise."

"Oh," said Mike, pretending disappointment.

She gave him a saucy look. "Doesn't mean it's not on the cards for tonight, though."

Mike's skin heated at her expression. He wasn't sure he could wait until later. It had been too long since he'd been inside her. He reminded himself her parents were in the next room, but it barely dampened his desire for her.

"So what's this surprise?" His voice was rough in his throat.

Jessica stood back so he could see her more clearly. Then, she pointed to herself, crossed her arms over her chest with her hands in fists, and finally put her hand out towards him as if offering him a platter.

I. Love. You.

Mike's heart kicked and his breath was trapped in his throat. "You learned it in sign," he whispered. She'd even learned the more intimate version of the phrase, since there was a more casual way to say it. He hoped to God that was on purpose.

She smiled at him. "You said there was less chance of confusion with sign language. And I didn't want you to have any doubt about what I felt for you."

Mike let out an unsteady breath, and then snatched Jessica into his arms. He kissed her fiercely, tenderly, letting all his emotions pour into the kiss.

Jessica was safe, in his arms.

And he wouldn't ever let her go.

Also by the author:

Underground Fighters Series

Caged Warrior
Russian Beast
Undercover Fighter

ABOUT THE AUTHOR

Wounded Heroes. Action Movies. Happily Ever Afters.

These are a few of Aislinn's favourite things, and you'll find all of the above in her writing. Whether it's the Soldiering On series – about wounded military veterans starting a security company together and finding love along the way – or her series about underground fighters.

If she's not reading romance novels or watching action movies, you'll find Aislinn writing like mad to get the next book out. She also loves to travel to new places around the world, forever in search of the perfect cottage in the forest that she hopes to one day call home.

Visit her at:
https://aislinnkearns.com/
Follow on Facebook at:
www.facebook.com/aislinn.kearns.writer
Twitter:
www.twitter.com/ardentaislinn
And Goodreads:
https://www.goodreads.com/author/show/15428911.Aislinn_Kearns

Printed in Great Britain
by Amazon